Dark Secret

Deadly Romance in the French Countryside

Lizzie Diamond

Source ISBN: 978-1-7391799-2-2
Ebook Edition © September 2022
ISBN: 978-1-7391799-0-8
Paperback Edition © September 2022

Cover design by: Gina Bertoldi

To all the dogs who have maintained my emotional stability throughout my turbulent life.

Gone but not forgotten, forever in my heart, always by my side.

Contents

Title Page
Copyright
Dedication
Chapter 1 1
Chapter 2 9
Chapter 3 13
Chapter 4 18
Chapter 5 30
Chapter 6 44
Chapter 7 53
Chapter 8 63
Chapter 9 74
Chapter 10 84
Chapter 11 91
Chapter 12 104
Chapter 13 116

Chapter 14	125
Chapter 15	137
Chapter 16	143
Chapter 17	154
Chapter 18	161
Chapter 19	169
Chapter 20	179
Chapter 21	187
Chapter 22	196
Chapter 23	203
Chapter 24	208
Chapter 25	218
Chapter 26	226
The Confession	229
Chapter 27	239
Epilogue	243
Preview	260
Acknowledgement	263
About The Author	265

Chapter 1

Alexandra Taylor parked her car outside the bakery in the sleepy country town of Lassay-les-Châteaux and went in to buy an almond croissant. She had been craving them for the last hour as she sped towards her parents' holiday home, a converted farmhouse tucked away in the heart of the French countryside.

Alex had taken the overnight ferry from Portsmouth to Caen and made the mistake of not booking a cabin. She had attempted to get as comfortable as possible in the supposedly reclining chair, wrapping her chunky cardigan around her to keep warm.

She wished she had been better prepared like some of the more seasoned travellers, who had stretched out on the floor with pillows and sleeping bags. Yet nothing could have cut through the discomfort of sharing an open space with fifty other passengers, surrounded by the snoring, coughing and smell of all those bodies trying to get a good night's sleep on their way to France.

Alex drove through the pretty Normandy

countryside with its green fields, winding roads and ancient stone cottages. She tried not to think too much about the last time she had done this trip, the previous summer with John for her parents' 30th wedding anniversary.

That was a different time when she still had a dream that one day it would be her and John; happily married for many years, surrounded by their children, content to be celebrating their life together. Well, it wasn't going to happen.

John represented everything she had thought she wanted in a partner; attractive, loyal, responsible. He owned his flat and had a well-paying job, and ticked all the boxes as far as her parents were concerned. He would have made a wonderful father and husband, but he could be overly controlling. He was undemonstrative and emotionally reserved, and she wondered if he was even truly interested in her at all.

Alex had done everything she could to compromise, see his point of view, not push things; but she couldn't live with the constant disappointment. She watched as one by one her friends got married, and envied their happiness as their babies started to arrive. She had dropped the biggest hints but eventually she had to give John an ultimatum.

She wanted more and she had reached the limit of her patience after three years living at his place.

Couldn't they at least buy their own home? Maybe as a project? Something to achieve and build a future together? He still wouldn't commit to anything; it was hard enough to get him to discuss it even, and now they had broken up and she had moved out and that was that. She was alone and single again, but she was almost certain it was the right choice.

Alex remembered her life before John; the party days of dancing until dawn, losing yourself in the music, hanging out with friends, flying off on last-minute holidays. Life with John was safe, but there was no place for letting your hair down or going off the route mapped out by him. He was predictable to the point of dull, and if she was honest with herself, John had never really made her happy.

She was tired from lack of sleep plus the long hours of driving, and was looking forward to the next few weeks of sanctuary at her parents' farmhouse. She wanted to put on her pyjamas, watch movies and eat fattening French food. She would lie in the garden on the lounger with a bottle of wine, a good book and sunshine on her face.

***

As far as Alex was concerned, her favourite *boulangerie* in Lassay was one of the wonders of the world. Six days a week, from dawn to dusk, its doors opened to the heady aroma of freshly baked bread. There was a magnificent display of various baguettes, brown loaves, delicious croissants with chocolate and almonds, indulgent cakes and colourful fruit tarts. All these delights lay spread out behind glass screens to be admired. Everything was made from scratch on the premises and presented with the flair and pride of a true artisan.

It was mid-morning by the time Alex arrived at her destination. There was a short queue of people spilling out onto the pavement waiting to purchase their daily bread. Alex fished in her bag for her purse, then stared at the back of a tall blonde guy standing in front of her in the queue.

Alex had come to Lassay to escape thinking about men, but she couldn't help but notice the contours of his muscular shoulders under a close-fitting white shirt. He had the strong, athletic build of a man comfortable with himself and his place in the world. Wow, Lassay had gained a good-looking one.

As he turned round to leave, he gave her a brilliant smile showing perfect white teeth and clear blue eyes.

"*Excuse-moi mademoiselle*," he smiled as he caught her gazing at him and for a second, she felt flustered.

He immediately turned his attention to an older

lady behind her, whom he greeted by kissing on both cheeks. As far as Alex could tell, the man sounded French, but something about his body language didn't look native. His confident demeanour made him appear very different from the locals, as if he owned the place rather than belonging there.

Alex completely forgot every word of French she had ever known and had to point to what she wanted, tipping a handful of coins out of her purse so the assistant could count out the right amount. She hurried out of the shop but instead of getting straight into her car, she found herself watching as this handsome mystery man sauntered, relaxed and assured, up the street towards the centre of town.

Alex took the road towards her parents' farmhouse past the two beautiful 18th century houses that sat at the edge of town. She knew that this type of imposing mansion, known as a *maison de bourg,* typically belonged to Brits who had bought them for a bargain price. They soon found out the hard way exactly how expensive such properties were to maintain and why local French people did not rush to buy them, but both of these were stunning examples and had been well-maintained with lots of care as well as cash.

It was a glorious summer day and she couldn't wait to cover the last few kilometres and get to the house. The road curved and there it was, nestled in the green fields, the second home her parents had owned for the past ten years. It was so familiar and so typically French.

As Alex drove into the courtyard, she let it all seep in; the warm walls of local stone covered in wisteria and climbing white roses, hanging baskets filled with geraniums and lobelia, hand-painted pots of lilies and lavender. The drive and the courtyard were protected by tall oaks and gleaming silver birches, with flowering shrubs marking the boundaries of the organic farm next door.

Alex parked her car in the open garage, got out and let the balmy June sunshine wash over her face as she stretched her limbs after the long drive. She took her suitcase out of the boot and opened the front door with the strangely large and heavy iron key that seemed to belong to a different age. She dropped her bag in the hall and walked through to the kitchen, the heart of any farmhouse.

When her mother had agreed that she could stay for a while, she had telephoned in advance their cleaning lady and had the house aired, cleaned and fresh bedding put in the master suite. She was so glad to escape and come here, where she could get away from all her cares and feel like she was truly home.

Alex made a large cup of coffee and took her

croissant out onto the terrace, where she sat on a painted oak bench and felt all the tension and stress of the past few weeks and the long journey drain away. She briefly considered the good-looking young man in the bakery and put the thought away. No Alex, you don't need any more complications, she told herself.

She checked her mobile phone to see if she had any messages. None from John, she wondered what he was doing now? At work most likely. She missed the routine and normality of their life together; her new place felt lonely without him.

There was one message from her boss at work, she would text him later. She felt bad about the lies she had told to justify her absence but honestly, her job working in a small publishing company wasn't going anywhere.

She had pretended that her grandmother was sick and that she had to go to France and help her grandfather look after her. This had not gone down too well, but Alex had insisted that there was no one else available to take on this responsibility. Eventually they had let her go and wished her the best, hoping it was not too serious and she would return soon. These good wishes made Alex feel uncomfortable, but for once in her life she was determined to put herself first.

She was suffocating from a lifetime of pleasing others and yet constantly nagged by the feeling of never being good enough. She knew she had made the right choice; no more waiting, no more false hope. She had tried so hard to be the woman that John wanted, but it had not been enough to secure the commitment she needed from him. Alex craved this escape; it would soothe her broken heart, ease her soul and help her recover.

Chapter 2

Xavier de Verre sat outside on the terrace of his new house and luxuriated in his feeling of well-being. This was the only property he had ever owned, his first real home. He had previously rented a small studio in Paris, just a place for sleeping and throwing the odd hasty meal together. Otherwise, he spent all his time working as the front man for a television nature programme *Le Monde Naturel*, which translated as 'The Natural World'.

At first, he'd had to prove himself as an exciting and knowledgeable naturalist and this had not been easy. He knew his subject expertly and could communicate with passion and charisma. As an extremely good-looking young man from a wealthy and prominent family, well-known and influential on the political circuit, it was difficult for people to take him seriously. They thought he was just another product of nepotism, a playboy wanting fame, but he was nothing like that.

Xavier's father was a career politician, absent and distant all through his young life. Although he loved his mother, famous in her own right as a model and socialite, he had soon learnt never to rely on them being there for him. He was sent to exclusive boarding schools which did nothing to ease his loneliness, despite the constant company of other students. He frequently retreated into his imagination and memories of all the times when he had been truly happy.

He could recall his childhood holidays at the family villa in Saint-Jean-Cap-Ferrat, where his parents had retreated every August for the summer break. It was here that he discovered the richness and variety of the natural world. Later he went to the University of Montpellier to study natural sciences. He loved France and was able to bring to life his passion for nature by studying the wildlife of his native country.

The television programme would probably never have happened without his parents' connections, or at least Xavier may not have been chosen as the presenter without the cachet of his famous name, but the show *Le Monde Naturel* had proven to be popular and he had risen like a reluctant star.

Now he was in the third year of filming and there was talk that Paramount Television was going to buy the first series and take it to the American audience, much like the great French naturalist Jacques Cousteau. Cousteau had studied and filmed marine life, but Xavier focused on the land and if Paramount launched this, it could make Xavier a global star, the same way American television had made Cousteau an international sensation.

Reflecting on his new acquisition, buying this house from his English friend Sarah had felt like a step he wasn't quite ready to make. When Sarah Jones had telephoned him six months ago and told him her contract with the BBC had run out and she was overstretched financially, his heart had told him to buy her 18th century *maison de bourg* on the outskirts of Lassay.

Xavier had driven the three hours from Paris the year before for Sarah's 50th birthday celebrations, and had been enchanted by the painstaking renovations she had undertaken. The house had not been just renovated, it had been restored to its former glory; and who better to accomplish this than Sarah, a specialist in historic re-creations for the film and television industry. The house was a triumph; she had bought it for next to nothing, the project was overwhelming, but the results were spectacular.

Now Xavier was here in his outstanding eight-bedroomed country home looking over his stunning garden. He pulled the cork on a bottle of excellent chilled chablis and savoured the moment. He had many messages left unread on his mobile, but he had told all his friends and professional colleagues that he was off the radar for the summer. Xavier knew he had not made a mistake buying the house but he would have liked to share this moment with someone, but with whom he did not know.

His mother made sure that he was not short of female company, but none of the pampered socialites she introduced him to had ever made him feel anything more than lust or temporary curiosity. He was not sure if he could feel more, and certainly his own family were not a source of inspiration. His beautiful mother was on her third husband and treated all of them like an open cheque book. His father was a professional workaholic with a neglected wife who was twenty years his junior.

Xavier had escaped into his studies at eighteen and had never quite connected again. The complicated world of romance and relationships, with all the rules, expectations and eventual discord, seemed fraught and confusing compared to the simplicity, grace and beauty of the natural world. It was not that he was so serious, nor was his heart closed to the idea of being in love, but he had never met anyone special enough.

Chapter 3

Elaine Dubois looked out of the shop window onto the little town square and dreamed of Paris. There was nothing to keep her in Lassay, she could leave anytime; but she didn't have enough money to start over somewhere else. Elaine had only ever known Lassay; she was born here, she grew up here, all her family lived here.

Her sister was married to a local farmer and had two adorable little girls, her brother was the chief of the local gendarmerie, and her parents' farm was less than three kilometres outside the town. Lassay was the limit of her life.

How would she ever get away? She knew she didn't belong here. At twenty-two, she should have already found a partner and be planning her wedding, but she didn't want to marry any of the country boys she had grown up with. Not that she wasn't popular, at 5'2" and a tiny size eight, with thick black hair falling in a modern cut over the biggest green eyes, she was stunning.

She had worked for the last two years in the local hairdressers and had as many male as female clients. Her customers liked her, they were attracted by her lively character and warm smile. Men certainly felt drawn to her and conversation came easily. She was always talking of faraway places and spent her free time in the shop thumbing through travel brochures and planning exotic trips she never took; but she would one day, she was sure of that.

Elaine was bored with no clients, gazing out the window at not much; everything she saw seemed so mundane and tediously familiar. People posting a letter in the yellow box outside the town hall, disappearing into the pharmacy to get their medicines; some headed over to the tabac to buy cigarettes, or maybe even chat with a friend over a coffee or glass of beer. One by one they all went away, and nothing ever really happened and it seemed that nothing ever would.

She had seen the forecast and was pleased it was going to be hot this weekend. Saturday was the annual outdoor painting event, when artists of every skill and style placed their easels in the streets and painted whatever they saw around them. It always drew a good crowd, and not just the local people. Perhaps someone would notice her and open the door to her escape.

Elaine was thinking about what she could wear to attract some attention, when a beautiful woman she had never seen before walked in. She noticed her gorgeous but unkempt, long blonde hair and couldn't wait to get to work. Elaine went straight over to welcome her with an engaging smile.

The woman looked uncertain as she tried to explain in halting French that she wanted an appointment, was it necessary to book in advance? Elaine immediately realised that she was English and was happy to show off her ability to speak her language.

At the local middle school, she had been in class with a girl whose parents had, for some unfathomable reason, left the bright lights of London to live in the countryside in the middle of nowhere. Always quick to take up any opportunity that might help her leave Lassay, Elaine had made sure that they became friends and she practiced her English and became quite fluent over the years.

"Come and sit down," Elaine invited her, handing her a new customer card to fill out. "You want me to cut and style?"

"No, no," replied Alex. "Just a tidy up. Is that ok?"

"Of course, no problem," Elaine smiled reassuringly.

Alex sat down and let Elaine run her experienced fingers through her strawberry-blonde hair, assessing the texture and condition.

"It's a bit sec, you know, dry. I'll give you a small cut

and a special treatment, ok? Are you living here?" Elaine asked.

"No, I'm just staying at my parents' holiday home for a few weeks, taking a break from London life," Alex offered, reluctant to get into further explanations of her heartbreak with this charming stranger.

"Oh, I had a friend who came from London. I went there once with my college and I tell you, if I lived in London, I'd never need to take a break," Elaine finished emphatically.

"Maybe, but we all need a change of pace sometimes," Alex replied.

"No, not me. If I go any slower, I will fall over and die!"

They warmed to each other and spent the next couple of hours chatting about places Alex had visited and Elaine had only dreamed of. The conversation switched to men and Alex unbuttoned a little about her recent break-up and Elaine was sympathetic.

By the time she was finished, Alex felt pampered and unusually glamorous, her naturally wavy hair now poker straight, sleek and shiny, hanging half-way down her back. Elaine was holding a mirror to show how the cut looked from behind.

"You like?" Elaine asked anxiously.

Alex loved it. The style really showcased her high cheekbones and almond-shaped hazel eyes. Combined with that fresh hair feeling, she was starting to feel special again. She kept glancing in the mirror, impressed despite herself at the stunning woman who stared back, barely recognisable from her usual natural look.

She left Elaine a generous ten euros tip and was just about to leave, when she noticed the poster pinned on the wall near the door advertising the annual outdoor painting day in the streets of Lassay. She stopped to look and saw that it was tomorrow.

“They have this every year at the beginning of June,” Elaine explained. “Why don’t you come along? It’s a good day, lots of people come to watch. I’ll be there in the afternoon, either looking at the pictures or sitting outside the Victor pub with some friends. I will keep an eye out for you. Remember, I’m Elaine.”

“Thank you, I might see you tomorrow. Bye,” she smiled.

Getting involved in socialising with new people, plus the possible complications they brought with them, was not at all what Alex had in mind.

Chapter 4

The first Saturday in June came in sizzling hot. Alex sat outside on the terrace and had her coffee, but even by 10.00am she knew it would be a scorcher. Fresh air combined with freedom from having to think about anyone but herself had invigorated her. Alex took a quick shower, threw on a floral print, cotton summer dress, brushed her long hair and picked up a shopping bag.

She drove into Lassay to buy her bread from the bakery and a few things she needed from Huit à Huit, the small supermarket in the town square that certainly never opened from 8.00am in the morning until 8.00pm at night. The name had always been a source of amusement to the Brits used to all day every day, plus late-night shopping. She picked up some cheese, ham and salad for a basic meal later, glad not to have to use too much of her limited language.

"*Au revoir, bonne journée*," she smiled the standard response of 'goodbye, good day' as she left the shop.

It was an idyllic, quintessentially French scene as

she looked out over the square now buzzing with people. Some of the artists were setting up their easels and canvases. They seemed well-prepared, many with small tables and brightly-coloured sunshades to protect them from the relentless heat.

She strolled to the local tabac and sat at one of the tables outside in the shade. The scene had a dreamlike quality and she was observing the people walking by, when a shadow blocked the sun and a figure appeared in front of her.

"Hello, I hope I'm not bothering you. I'm Jack Winter," a voice said. It was the cute guy from the bakery.

"Oh, hi. I'm Alex Taylor, do I look English?" Alex accepted Jack's outstretched hand. "I feel as if everyone can tell."

"I know," said Jack. "It's what we do here for sport, it's called 'spot the Brit'. I saw you the other day in the bakery. Can I buy you a coffee?"

"Thank you, Jack, that would be nice," she replied, flattered by him singling her out.

Jack went inside to order and Alex smiled to herself. Well what about that, she'd picked up the hunk. There was life after John.

Jack returned a few minutes later and pulled his chair beside her so they could both look out at the scene. Expertly and unnoticed, Jack instantly assessed this opportunity; no engagement or wedding ring, sensuous perfume but no make-up, probably not on the pull. A challenge, but he was up for that. She was the first to speak.

“Do you live here Jack?”

“Well sort of, I look after the only hotel in town for my uncle, he’s had loads of staffing problems. Last year I was at a loose end so I packed up and came down here for the summer, which kind of ran into the winter and hey, all of a sudden, the summer is here again. What about you? What’s your reason for being in such a small town?”

“My parents own a holiday home here and I needed a quiet break,” she offered. It just would not do to be dumping her troubles on a stranger, particularly such a handsome one.

“Where are you from in the UK, Alex?” he asked.

“London, just by Putney Bridge,” she added.

“We must have nearly been neighbours. I lived in Chelsea before I came here,” he dropped in to impress her. “Listen I’ve got to rush, I’ve no receptionist at the moment,” he said, draining his small black coffee and standing up.

“Are you coming back later? I’ll buy you a beer in the Victor and we can criticize their efforts,” he nodded towards the artists diligently working. There were about twenty painters now determined to make a day of it and show off their talents.

"Maybe, I'll see how I go. Thank you for the coffee Jack, bye for now," she replied.

With a kiss on each cheek in the French manner, the charming Jack Winter went back to his hotel pleased with himself for meeting the beautiful Alex Taylor. He was definitely intending to see her again.

Alex was not sure if she wanted to meet up with Elaine, or Jack for that matter. He was certainly attractive but this sort of summer fling was the last thing she needed.

It was too hot to sit outside now, although she felt reluctant to head straight home. Unlike the English houses she had grown up in, the farmhouse was cold and dark inside. This was a deliberate and clever design aspect to make it cool in the long hot summers. Although supremely appropriate for a day like this, it made her feel gloomy so she decided to take a wander around town before heading back.

Lassay was the busiest she had ever seen it and more people arriving by the minute. Every parking space in the town centre was full, with cars now lining the side streets. The cafés and bars were doing a roaring trade with visitors come to see the painting and any excuse for a festive occasion.

Alex walked towards the crowd, stopping every now and then to look over the shoulder of a working artist, struggling to capture the moment. They were hoping to win one of the prizes on offer at the end of the day when all the work was handed in for judging.

She contemplated buying a piece for her mother as a thank you for letting her stay in the house. She started to observe the artists' technique, really looking at each painting and time slipped away unnoticed.

She was watching along with a crowd, as a flamboyant woman in flowing skirts and a gypsy top covered in paint, put the finishing touches to a Monet-like rendition of the 12th century medieval château across the lake. This artist in particular had captured the style and history of the graceful scene she had chosen with care, despite working from a photo, as the château was just out of sight from the town square.

It was an especially beautiful and famous château, built in the rich-coloured stone of the region that was found throughout the village and in many, if not all, of the farmhouses. Lassay in fact boasted three famous castles but the one near the town centre was a stunning example, although needing constant maintenance.

This was the reason for the name Lassay-les-Châteaux and it was a picture postcard village. It had been the centre of the salt trade between Brittany, Normandy and France where the ancient countries had met, and had evolved into an important trading point.

She was wondering what price she could offer to buy this picture and the exact protocol for that, when she felt Jack Winter's face very close to hers across her shoulder.

"Not bad, what do you think?" he asked.

Alex tried to move her head but not before Jack had planted a big kiss on her cheek, in a rather too familiar way for someone she had only just met.

"Oh, hi Jack. I was thinking that too," she replied, turning to put some space between them. "I was wondering how much it would cost. I might buy it for my parents' house."

"Wait for the judging at 7.00pm in the *salle des fêtes*, that's the social hall near the château. You'll be able to compare them when you see the finished results," he suggested. "It's been a beautiful day but it's a bit hot to be wandering around. How about a cold beer? What do you think, Mademoiselle Taylor?"

"Ok, why not?" Alex suddenly realised she was very hot and thirsty and a cold beer sounded delicious. "Do you think we'll be able to get a seat? It looked pretty packed as I walked past earlier."

"Leave it to Jack," he smiled confidently.

Amazingly, as they arrived at the Victor pub, a group of people left the bench table outside and wandered off to look at the paintings.

"There you go, perfect, and just a bit jammy of course!" he smirked, looking for the waiter.

Suddenly Elaine came scooting across the square, waving and smiling.

"*Bonjour* Alex," she gushed, happy to see her. Alex stood to receive the mandatory kisses on each cheek.

"*Bonjour* Jack," she smiled, giving him the four kisses usually reserved for close friends and family.

"*Comment ça va, chérie*?" Jack sat down after the standard greeting of 'how are you?', but Alex could tell from the '*chérie*' meaning 'darling', that they definitely did know each other, perhaps intimately.

Elaine and Jack started talking together amicably in French, pleased to have run into each other. Maybe they were just old friends, Alex thought. She wasn't really interested in Jack, but she was impressed by the way he could just switch with no effort into the language. She tried to follow the conversation concentrating hard on each word to pick up the gist of their exchange.

Elaine was clearly joining them as she squeezed herself onto the bench next to Alex. Jack finally caught the attention of the waiter and ordered.

"You like?" she asked Jack, pointing to Alex's hair.

"Very much," he replied, smiling at Alex and making her feel slightly uncomfortable.

Jack and Elaine continued to chat easily together, mostly in French, but occasionally offering translations for Alex's benefit. Alex had been drifting in and out of the conversation, not really listening and waiting for the right opportunity to leave, when suddenly Elaine got very excited.

"Look, look over there. It's Xavier de Verre! Oh look, isn't he wonderful? I can't believe it's him! Here in Lassay, oh my God! What do I look like?" she turned to Alex.

"You look great, Elaine," Alex assured her truthfully.

Following the other girl's gaze, she caught sight of the most beautiful man walking slowly towards them. She guessed he was in his mid-thirties, tall and bronzed with dark hair worn casually long. Alex wondered if he was some French film star that she had never heard of, as he caused many heads to turn.

"Who is he?"

"My God Alex, don't you know? It's Xavier de Verre," she gushed. "He's just about the best-looking man on television, wouldn't you say Jack?"

"Strangely Elaine, I can't really see the attraction myself," he replied.

"Move up Jack, make a space. He might be coming here for a drink. Oh please God, let him be very, very thirsty," she prayed, as she pulled herself up provocatively to catch his attention.

Jack reluctantly shifted along the bench whilst both girls stared.

"I can't believe you don't know who he is Alex," Elaine was amazed. "He presents some boring programme that my parents like about wildlife, but it's worth watching just to see him strip off and swim with fishy things. I think they send him to the rivers and lakes on purpose to get his shirt off every week, talking about frogs and other vile little creatures. He's got a body to die for and that's all I need to know!"

Elaine grew misty-eyed with lust and fell silent, desperately willing Xavier to notice her. Alex could understand exactly, she found she couldn't take her eyes off him. She could hardly breathe as he kept walking over, getting closer by the second, until eventually he stood directly in front of them.

Xavier stared straight at Alex, who felt like a rabbit caught in headlights. She noticed his eyes were bright blue in the sunshine and her heart skipped a beat. This Adonis of a man bowed slightly and in a perfect, deep French voice asked if he could join their table.

Elaine jumped up, fixed him with her green eyes and her most captivating smile and took the lead introducing him to the others. Taking a seat, he seemed slightly amused as he shook hands and offered to buy them all another beer.

Elaine positively radiated interest and fixed her attention exclusively on Xavier. Rapid French conversation followed and Alex got completely lost whilst the others chatted and made small-talk. Suddenly Xavier looked directly at Alex and asked her a question she didn't quite catch. She fumbled her attempt to ask him to repeat it and gave herself away.

"You're English?" he asked.

"Yes. Sorry my French is not so good," she blushed apologetically.

"That's ok, I like to practice my English when I can," he smiled. Xavier only had eyes for her.

Elaine was not going to let that happen and she continued to talk exclusively to Xavier in French, demanding his attention. Jack became unusually quiet, and Alex sensed that he felt put out. She was wondering how best to make her move and head home, but something about Xavier kept her rooted to the spot.

Alex tried not to look directly at him, she felt rather hot and uncomfortable every time their eyes met. Jack must have noticed this too because he drained his glass, leaned across the table, fixed Alex with a very direct look and made his move.

"So, Miss Taylor, when can I take you to lunch, or better still dinner?"

Alex felt taken aback. She had not expected that question, and all eyes turned towards her anticipating her answer.

"Sorry Jack, I'm not sure I'm ready just yet," she resented being put on the spot like that. It felt distinctly territorial and unpleasant with it.

"Hey, I wasn't asking for your hand in marriage," he said defensively. "I just thought you might like some company now and then, it's not important."

The atmosphere had changed and only Elaine seemed oblivious and continued to babble on to Xavier. She was determined not to miss her opportunity to impress the handsome celebrity. Alex wanted to get away so she made her excuses and stood up to leave. Jack still had not given up and offered to see her to the car.

"No really, I'll be fine," she insisted.

Alex did not do the kissing thing, she just said goodbye and headed off as quickly as possible. She needed to get home and retreat from the burgeoning sense of unwelcome entanglements.

Chapter 5

Alex arrived at her car and took a moment to collect herself before starting the drive home. She kept running through her head the whole episode at the Victor. It was one thing to feel bored, out of place or not understand the language, but something about Jack's abruptness and Xavier's drop-dead gorgeous presence had made her feel distinctly off and unsettled.

She sat in her car with her head in her hands for a few moments, taking deep breaths. The whole scene was so embarrassing, what was wrong with her? She felt like a gauche teenager, not a woman of twenty-eight who should have handled the situation better.

"Alex, are you ok? You seem upset."

She jumped at the sound of Xavier's voice at her open car window.

"Oh, Xavier, I'm so sorry. I'm just a bit overcome by the heat, I'm ok," she replied, trying to pull herself together.

"Which way do you go? Would you like me to

drive if you feel unwell?" he asked, with genuine concern.

"No, no really, I'll be fine. I only live a few kilometres out of town towards Javron so it's not far."

"Ah, then maybe you'd like to give me a lift. I live on your route home," he informed her.

"Yes of course, hop in," she offered.

Xavier walked round and took the passenger seat.

"It feels odd to be on this side with no steering wheel," he observed, as she took off in the direction of the farmhouse.

Alex focused on the road ahead, as she wondered what she was going to say to him. She had never even seen his show but just like Elaine, felt the female instinct to be attractive, witty and engaging; yet unlike the French girl, she had no idea how to make small-talk with this unknown celebrity with whom she had literally nothing in common.

She was somewhat shocked by her strong physical reaction to his masculine presence, and could understand exactly why Jack would have been disturbed by this very big fish arriving in his small pool.

"You were made uncomfortable by Jack's

proposition?" he broached, as if he had read her mind. "I thought perhaps he was your boyfriend?"

"Definitely not," Alex shook her head. "I hardly know him. I only met him today, but you know, us Brits tend to stick together as our French is so bad."

"Elaine made it very clear she was available!" Xavier commented and they both smiled at that.

"I think she's rather star-struck, don't you? I'm sure you have been in that position before." Alex was only too aware from her own response that most women would be highly attracted to him.

"Not too often, thankfully," he replied modestly.

It was unusual for a celebrity not to crave that sort of attention, Alex noted and approved, but said nothing. What did she know about such things? She was just trying to think of something interesting to reply, when Xavier surprised her after they had driven for literally only a minute or two.

"It's here on the right," he indicated the stunning *maison de bourg* just outside the village.

"That's the English lady's house, isn't it?" Alex asked.

"Not anymore, I bought it from her two weeks ago."

"It's the most beautiful house, I've always admired

it," Alex said reverently. "My mother loves it, we always wanted to look inside. We'd heard that it had been restored perfectly, not just the usual ripping everything out and making awful renovations."

"That's true," Xavier confirmed. "Sarah did a wonderful job, it's why I bought it. When I heard she wanted to sell, I jumped at the opportunity to own such a house."

"I can understand exactly why. It's magnificent, even from the road."

"Normally I rent just a small studio in Paris, it's all I need. I work all over the country and only get back to edit my series when filming is done. This is my first real home," Xavier explained.

They pulled into the driveway of the superb 18th century mansion. Alex admired the beautiful façade of the house that she had never seen this close before. It was the most stunning property in the village, perfect in proportions, set in walled grounds with a carefully-tended garden.

Xavier had not been able to resist the chance to own what he considered a piece of history; the skill and craftsmanship of his country evident throughout. He worked very hard and this was his prize, his reward, his place in the world. He felt proud to be the master of such a mansion and pleased to have a beautiful woman by his side to admire it after the solitude of his first night.

"Would you like to come in?" Xavier suggested.

"I'd love to, if it's not too inconvenient," Alex smiled.

She couldn't wait to get a look at the interior. She would telephone her mother later and explain all the details of the house they had both admired so often.

"Since you are my very first guest, I would be honoured to give you a guided tour," he offered, pleased by this unexpected arrival and all that she represented.

Xavier came round to open the car door for her before Alex had the chance to jump out. She was not used to anybody, especially John, displaying such charming manners, even if somewhat quaint and out-of-date by her standards. He was such a gentleman, she felt more like a character in a *Mills & Boon* novel by the second. This kind of thing simply did not happen to people in real life, surely?

Her unexpected crush on Xavier was forgotten when she stepped inside the house and was dazzled. The entrance was amazing, bigger than her family's whole farmhouse. There were exquisite Italian-tiled floors and the walls were panelled in delicate ivory silk. Her eyes were drawn to the sweeping, pale marble staircase that led to a balcony that encompassed the whole upper floor. The two full-size, original windows let the light flood in from the south-facing garden and fill the area with warm summer, afternoon light.

Alex was stunned by the overall impression of elegance and overwhelmed with the craftsmanship. It was just outstanding, everything she had dreamed it would be.

"It's so beautiful," was all she could manage, but Xavier could tell her instinctive response to the house mirrored his own feelings.

"I came here last year for Sarah's birthday party," Xavier explained. "She works in television as a set designer who specialises in historical programmes. She made her reputation with her attention to detail. Everybody was impressed by her insistence on perfection, but you can see why I had to have it, can't you?"

"I certainly can," replied Alex.

It took half an hour to give her the full tour. Alex could see how passionate Xavier was about the house and with good reason. Each room had been painstakingly restored, everything put back into its rightful place. Every piece of furniture chosen for authenticity and balance, no harsh colours just pearly white, cream and the palest oyster everywhere.

"Can I offer you a glass of cold chablis on the terrace?" Xavier asked.

It had slipped his mind before because she had been so entranced by the house, and he had been delighted to show it off to such a rapt, appreciative guest.

“Please take a seat,” he said, leading her outside.

There was an antique, white metal table and chairs for formal entertaining but he pointed to the more comfortable outdoor seating area for her to relax in, before disappearing to get the wine.

Alex sat and breathed in the late afternoon sunshine, admiring everything she saw in the private walled garden. The lawn was flawless, well-tended plants on display, with roses and clematis climbing on trellis and various arches and features.

Clearly this was the work of a professional gardener, it must cost a fortune to keep up to this standard. Handsome, rich, famous and far too out of her league for the daydreams that kept entering her head. Alex could barely imagine herself living this life with a prince like Xavier, but for the moment it was heaven.

Xavier returned after a minute with two glasses, an ice bucket and a chilled bottle of chablis.

“Do you feel a little better?” he asked.

“I feel much better. Thank you, Xavier,” she told

him. "You've managed to save an increasingly deteriorating day. I'm so grateful."

They sat for a moment in companionable silence.

"I am glad you followed me," she confessed, without any forethought, but her tone came out huskier than usual.

"I'm glad too," he held her eyes that extra moment longer.

"I have to admit I noticed you before I came over to the table," he went on. "I'm not usually so forward but I wanted to meet you. Mostly people tend to assume I'm rude and arrogant, but I'm kind of shy. I like privacy and my own company, because that is what I am used to. I am lucky I got into filming and I love what I do. France is a beautiful and diverse country and I'm happy to reveal the incredible wildlife so people can see these things for themselves."

Xavier fell silent for a few moments and seemed deep in thought.

"Why are you here alone, Alex?" he ventured.

Alex took some time to consider her response, not wanting to say anything to ruin the moment.

"It's a long story but simply, without wanting to bore you with the details; a broken relationship, a stressful job, the commute to work, all of those things in that order," she said firmly.

Xavier understood. He was aware from the determined look on her face she would not want to be pressed further. A broken relationship was just that and no more questions were needed.

"We should eat," he stood up, smoothing down his shirt and smiling at her.

"Please don't go to any trouble, I've probably outstayed my welcome. I certainly won't be able to drive if I drink anymore today," Alex protested, as he poured the last of the wine equally into the two glasses.

"I hate to eat alone and I'm an excellent cook," he insisted. "If you want to stay, you can see I have eight bedrooms to choose from, that is, if you trust me?"

Alex could feel her heart beating in her chest as his blue eyes looked questioningly at her, loaded with deeper meanings and intention. She knew she should leave now, that would be the sensible thing to do. He saved her having to answer by walking inside, so she followed him through to the kitchen and watched as he pulled things out of the cupboards and fridge.

"Let me help, please, just tell me what to do. I can take orders and try not to get in the way."

Alex made up her mind; life was for living and

this chance was too good to miss. If the universe had given her this gift, then she was determined to enjoy every minute of the fantasy as long as it lasted.

"Ok, in the cupboard over there you'll find the table setting, would you mind taking care of it?" Xavier pointed. "That would be helpful, thanks. We'll eat outside."

It was still wonderfully warm and balmy in the evening sunlight. Alex busied herself setting the table, going back and forth between the kitchen and the terrace; taking things through as Xavier passed them to her, including a bowl of olives to pick on whilst he finished the delicious-smelling pasta, grated with fresh parmesan and a green salad.

It all looked amazing and Alex realised she had spent most of the day in the sun drinking and had eaten nothing. She was starving in fact, although she hadn't noticed until now. Maybe that was what she could feel inside her; not a fluttering heart, just hunger pangs.

When Xavier joined her on the terrace with another bottle of chablis, his linen shirt unbuttoned and his smooth brown chest exposed to reveal splendid rippling muscles, she felt her throat constrict. The beating got louder and it was definitely in her chest and not her stomach, in fact she wasn't even sure she was hungry anymore, or if she would even be able to stand up if she needed to.

Alex had never, ever felt like this before. She was completely bewitched, light-headed from the wine, hot and flustered, as he looked at her with his bright blue eyes and an intimate smile.

"You are beautiful, Alex. This setting is perfect for you. You've made me so happy by allowing me to entertain you and share this evening." He filled the glasses again and proposed a toast.

"To new friendships," he said, instead of the usual French '*santé*', meaning 'to your health'.

"To new friendships," she repeated.

Something told her it would be very hard keeping Xavier as just a friend, and couldn't help but offer a secret wish that he would fall madly in love with her. What had got into her? Would she turn into one of those people who didn't believe in love at first sight, only to find it like magic and be proven totally, wonderfully wrong?

As the sun started to set and the wine kept flowing, a warm darkness enveloped them. They sat together and chatted easily about their work, their likes and dislikes, their childhoods. Xavier carefully avoided any awkward questions about the previous relationship she had mentioned. Alex found herself relaxing more in his company and he was charming and humorous; she even laughed out loud a few times, before she realised she was indeed quite drunk.

Xavier got up to make some coffee and clear away the last of the plates from the table. Alex rested her head for a few moments on her crossed arms, closed her eyes and within seconds she had fallen into a deep sleep.

When Xavier returned with the coffee, he gently touched her bare arm. She didn't move, so he stroked her golden hair but she remained still. He drank his coffee quietly and looked at her, watching her sleeping peacefully. She was such a beautiful and charming woman, so refreshingly natural. It had been a long time since he had felt so comfortable in female company.

It was true that many women admired him, but he was very selective and preferred to be alone with his books and research than chasing women for the sake of it. Often when he was filming, the crew went out in search of excitement after a long day, but he rarely joined them which just added to their opinions that he was aloof and arrogant.

Alex changed position trying to get more comfortable. He put his face very close to hers and could smell the last hints of her perfume.

"Alex," he whispered in her ear. "Let me help you. Come on, can you stand?"

Alex shifted again but there was no further

reaction.

"*Chérie*, put your arm around my neck and I'll lift you," he said more forcefully, but still no response.

Xavier carefully placed her limp arm around his neck and with strong muscles lifted her in one easy sweep. She wasn't heavy, she just nestled comfortably in his arms as he carried her up the marble staircase to his room. He was thrilled at how perfect this felt with her head against his half-bare chest. He was not wrong about this girl; she was something special and he didn't intend to let her get away.

It was true he had eight bedrooms, but only one bed was made up with linen and that was his. He lay her very carefully down on top of the quilt without turning on the lights. Her shoes had fallen from her feet on the ascent, but she wouldn't need them tonight. He returned to the ground floor where he tidied and locked up his house, then quietly went back up to the bedroom.

He took off his shirt and lay down on the bed next to her, watching her breathing in the darkness. He considered taking off her summer dress, but he was certain this was beyond her boundaries and would make her uncomfortable in the morning. He wasn't going to touch her; he didn't want to take such an easy advantage. She turned and draped her arm across his shoulder and moved closer, until her head was once again nestled against his naked chest.

Be careful, he told himself, one wrong move and you'll ruin this. He wished that the rest of his body was in the same state of control as his mind, but he couldn't stop himself from running his hand down the length of her back and resting lightly on her round bottom. He kissed the top of her head and tried to think of anything to distract himself from the painful swelling in his pants. Very gradually, after what seemed like an eternity, the gentle rhythm of her breathing lulled him to sleep.

Chapter 6

Alex started to become aware that she was pinned down by a strong arm. She tried to move but was enveloped by his warm body pressed perfectly into hers. Every part of her back was in contact with Xavier, even their feet were touching. She closed her eyes and desperately tried to remember getting into this position. What had she done?

She could not recall a single thing after she had rested her head for a few minutes on the table after the wonderful dinner. At least she was dressed so that was something, perhaps it wasn't too shameful after all.

She slowly lifted his arm and tried to slip away from his body, but he quickly replaced it and tightened his grip around her waist, pulling her closer to him. She instinctively wanted to turn around and press her lips to his, to feel the strength of his body on hers. She lay very still feeling every curve of his muscular frame wrapped around her. She could feel the blood flowing through her veins and an unbearable liquid heat in her groin. Had she ever been alive before now?

This was what real lust, real passion felt like; and it was different from anything she had ever experienced. She had to move or she'd explode; she was resisting her natural desires but her body seemed to be in a fever. Perhaps she was ill, she prayed she wouldn't be sick, but she couldn't bear listening to her pounding heart another minute. She had to get away so she jumped up, sprang off the bed and ran to the bathroom and locked the door.

Get a grip, she told herself, as she sat on the side of the bathtub. What the hell was happening to her? There was a knock and she heard Xavier's voice.

"Alex, are you sick?"

"No, I'm fine," she lied.

"Do you need anything? A glass of water or a coffee?" he sounded concerned.

"Coffee would be good," she answered.

Anything to get him to go away so she could pull herself together. She knew he would have to go downstairs to make the coffee and that would give her some time to shape up, look normal. Who are you kidding, Alex? You'll never be able to pull that one off, she thought.

After a brief check in the mirror, she was surprised at how well-rested she looked instead of the bedraggled mess she was anticipating. Once she had splashed her face with water and tidied her hair, she felt slightly more able to face him.

Alex descended the staircase, becoming aware from the cool marble sensation that her feet were bare. This gave her a jolt; the fact that she hadn't even noticed and had no idea where her shoes could be. She didn't care if she couldn't find them, she'd drive home barefoot if necessary. She just needed to get away and give herself time to recover.

She had lost most of her composure and was almost shaking as she paused outside the kitchen to gather her nerves. Either she had alcoholic poisoning or she was completely love-sick, there was no other explanation.

As she entered the kitchen, she hoped he wouldn't be able to see the turmoil reflected in her eyes. He was sitting at the kitchen table with a coffee in front of him reading a journal, a pair of black oblong glasses perched on the end of his nose. He lifted his blue eyes above the rims and looked straight at her. Oh God, I'm melting, she thought. She couldn't formulate any kind of sense in her head.

"Alex, *chérie*, you look so pale. Are you alright?"

"Too much wine," she managed to get out, but that was all.

He stood and came across to her, taking her face in his smooth hands, he kissed her ever so lightly on both sides.

"Come over here and sit down. Drink this, you'll feel better," he indicated a steaming espresso cup as he steered her towards the table.

She allowed herself to be led, relieved to be able to look away and into her coffee instead of his eyes. It was just the right temperature and exactly what she needed to face the drive home. Thank God it was only a few kilometres and soon this would all be over and she could get back to normality and her real life.

"Would you like me to run you a bath? It might help," Xavier offered, still the perfect gentleman. "I'm so sorry, it's my fault, I should have taken you home instead of insisting you stayed. Forgive me, I'm selfish, I didn't want the evening to end."

"Xavier, I do need to get home, freshen up, get changed." Alex stood up, she simply had to get away.

"Ok, no problem, I'll drive you. The walk back will do me good, it's not far you said."

Alex found her bag in the kitchen and handed Xavier the keys. She had put up no protest because she wasn't confident that she could manage it herself. She might be over the driving limit and the gendarmerie were always hiding in the bushes waiting for UK licence plates. She didn't even notice that she was still barefoot until she was in the car and half-way home, although she said nothing.

He parked the car in the courtyard of her parents' home and noticed her feet for the first time.

"Hey, your feet!" he laughed. "Wait there."

Xavier opened the car door for her and before she could say anything, had scooped her up and carried her across the gravel to the front door.

"This is becoming a habit, but one I like," he said, placing her on her feet and holding her for a few seconds too long.

"I'll go and leave you to it. You will come visit me another time?" he pressed.

"Yes, of course," she replied.

"Promise?" He was determined to see Alex again.

"I promise," she stated, desperately wanting him to go away.

Alex watched as he turned and headed up the drive. She was glad he had not tried to kiss her as she was in no state to resist. She could not believe what had happened and how she had ended up in an apparently innocent sleep-over, having passed out drunk in front of a famous man. He must be mad to want to see her again.

Xavier de Verre was definitely not what she needed, but how could anybody do anything but respond to that kind of star quality? The three C's: character, charisma, confidence. She was hooked, was there any point in fighting it? She was still staring as he turned and gave her a little wave, then she fumbled with the key and literally fell through the doorway into the hall.

Alex stayed on her hands and knees for some time, leaning forwards with her forehead resting on the cold tiled floor, letting the coolness seep into her head. When she felt strong enough to move, she went into the bathroom, stripped off and spent the next half-hour letting the water flow across her body and revive her. She dried off, put on one of her mother's fluffy, white terry-cloth bath robes, wrapped another towel around her hair and walked from the bathroom to the kitchen.

Alex stopped dead in her tracks. Jack Winter was sitting at her kitchen table with a coffee in his hand.

"God, Jack! You nearly gave me a heart attack!" she was shocked. "What on earth are you doing here? I was in the shower."

"I know Alex, I'm sorry," he said, sounding anything but.

"I didn't mean to scare you," he went on. "I called

out, but the front door was wide open and I could hear the water running. I thought you'd heard me and said it was ok. Please forgive me, I'm such an idiot. Look what I have for you," he said, holding up the Monet-like picture they had seen yesterday.

"I bought you the painting you were interested in," Jack held it out to her. "I hoped to see you at the judging but you weren't there, so I negotiated a great price and got it for you. Can it be a peace offering? I can see you're upset with me."

Alex was more than upset, she was absolutely furious. Suddenly she realised that she was standing half-naked in her kitchen with a relative stranger and decided to be diplomatic. She really could not handle any more scenes and just wanted him out of there as quickly as possible.

"Look that was very thoughtful, but really I must pay you for it," she insisted. "How much did it cost?"

"No please, it's a gift. One day maybe you'll forgive me for barging in here to give you a present," Jack smiled. "Also, for putting you on the spot yesterday when I asked you out. I didn't realise that you were recovering from a bad relationship. Elaine told me, I understand. I'll be more than happy if we can just be friends, at least for the time being."

Alex started to relax somewhat, before Jack

continued with his unwelcome compliments.

"I can't say I don't fancy you, Alex. You are a beautiful woman, any man with eyes in his head would want you."

"Ok Jack, now really, I have some things I need to do today and I have to get on." She was most uncomfortable and fed up with this intrusion.

If Jack had picked up the anger in her voice, he didn't show it but continued breezily, as though he and Alex were the warmest of friends.

"No problem, don't mind me. Shall I make you a coffee whilst you get dressed?" He seemed determined to be difficult. God, would he not just go away?

"No thank you, Jack," Alex replied as calmly as possible. "That's very considerate, but I think you should leave now. I'll catch up with you another time."

"Well, if you're sure. I'll go, but I'll call you later. Maybe we can have a drink in the pub?" he persisted.

Jack saw the reluctant look on Alex's face and decided to play his ace card.

"I know Elaine's gone round to see Xavier to invite him tonight. We could all get together and have a bit of a party. Elaine is determined to catch Xavier and let's face it, she's quite a babe and usually gets her man," he finished smugly, as if he had scored a point attempting to make her jealous. Surely he couldn't have known she had spent the night with Xavier?

Alex walked Jack to the door, and she remembered to lock it this time. She had nearly had a fit when she saw him sitting there, making himself at home. She knew people were kind of casual about dropping round in France and he seemed harmless enough, although definitely obnoxious. No, she'd just stay at home, keep quiet, that should calm things down a bit. She had no idea how wrong she was.

Chapter 7

Jack felt elated; he sensed the taste of romantic conquest ahead and relished the thrill of the chase. He would capture his prey, he was certain, it would all work out. This time he was sure and he would be patient, she was worth it. Alex had been a bit shocked to see him in her kitchen, he shouldn't have done that. It was a mistake, but he got away with it thanks to the painting.

Jack had many female friends and his pick of regular lovers from the local village women to the odd solo visitor staying at the hotel. He had created quite a stir amongst the fairer sex since arriving in Lassay. At 6'4", he towered over his French counterparts and had an undeniable air of confidence born out of the knowledge that not only was he good-looking, but he was intelligent and charming too when he wanted to be. He liked to flirt and tease and found no shortage of attention from the many women who came in and out of his life and his bed.

He had grown up in London with his French mother and two older sisters, in an atmosphere that was dominated by all things feminine. It was only when he was sixteen that his mother had married a wealthy stockbroker and things at home had started to go wrong. No longer the man of the house and too young to leave, he had set about trying to destroy his mother's marriage. Things got so bad that he had been sent to live with his natural father, step-mother and their three young children in Basingstoke.

It wasn't long before he had started to drop out of school and hang around in the park, smoke cannabis and get drunk at every opportunity. His father, a police inspector, was at his wits' end, especially when his colleagues started turning up on his doorstep at all hours asking questions about local petty crimes.

It had all blown up into a series of nasty scenes that had become increasingly more violent as time passed. Eventually after one of Jack's nightly binges, his father had given him a serious beating, breaking his nose and fracturing two ribs, and the next day he ran away. For a few months he hung out with friends, but he could not continue like that indefinitely.

When he met Marianne, a thirty-eight year old divorcée sitting alone in a local nightclub, insecure and rejected, he moved straight in and used his charm and body to live for free. It became a pattern; older women needed him for sex and adoration and he played the part to perfection. In return, he became the favoured son he had once been, pampered and spoilt.

These relationships never lasted but strangely it was usually the women who tired first. The sex, so important in the beginning to restore their confidence, became increasingly tiresome. As the novelty wore off, they soon realised Jack was as demanding a lover as he was person. With no real balance to the relationship, it became a one-way street; as their physical lust diminished and their interest started to wane, they gave in or gave up, tired of conflict.

There had only been one true love affair in his life and that was the pure love he felt for his mother. She had been taken away from him, he was determined that would never happen again. Alex would be different, he could feel it, with her he felt hope again.

***

Elaine went through the open gates and finding nobody home, sat on the steps of Xavier's house and waited. He couldn't be far away as his car, a black Porsche, was in the drive; he might have just nipped into town or be out walking somewhere.

Jack had dropped her off on his way to Alex's parents' farmhouse. Elaine had told Jack where Alex's house was and given him her number, he was so obviously smitten. It wasn't long ago that Elaine and Jack had been lovers, but she was pleased that they had both found somebody at the same time so there would be no rivalry.

No, Jack wasn't for Elaine; she liked him, he was good fun and could be very charming and his French was excellent. They had ended up in bed a few times after getting drunk together on a night out; but she needed somebody sensitive, who made love to her the French way and that definitely wasn't Jack.

Now Xavier, he was her dream come true. The thought of laying in Xavier's arms in this beautiful house; Elaine knew this was what she was born for, to live this life. It was another beautiful day so she decided to wait until he came back.

When Xavier found Elaine still on his doorstep, he was in excellent spirits and immediately invited her in for a coffee, kissing her twice on each cheek like an old friend. She was stunned by the size of the house and felt like a queen sitting on the terrace with Xavier. Elaine did not know that she was not the reason for his expansive mood, nor that she was in fact in exactly the same place that Alex had occupied only the night before.

They chatted easily about local places, then where to buy what he needed for his new home. Elaine volunteered her help; this was her region and he was a stranger. She was exactly the right person to take him shopping for whatever he required. She was so happy and enthusiastic that she failed to notice the strange look he gave her, after she suggested that the house would look much better when they had finished buying modern furnishings and re-decorated.

"I'd love to help," she continued. "Everything is so pale and old-fashioned; it definitely needs livening up."

Xavier just smiled and said nothing. She was very young, she obviously wouldn't understand. He decided it was time Elaine left, so he offered to give her a ride back to town. She was thrilled to travel in a Porsche, his one indulgence to the endless hours driving all over France for his work.

"It's the first time I have been in a car like this," Elaine was impressed.

As she directed him to the hotel in the centre of Lassay, she told Xavier that she was going out with Jack and Alex later to the local pub.

"Would you like to come with us?" She gave her most alluring smile but he was driving and missed it.

Normally he would have refused, but at the mention of Alex he impulsively decided to go along. It might be fun and he would like a chance to see her again so soon. He realised he had forgotten to give her his phone number. This seemed a perfect opportunity and as he dropped Elaine off, he agreed to meet them all later at the Victor at 9.00pm.

Elaine rushed into the hotel reception full of joy and straight into Jack. She was extremely pleased with the way her plans had come together and found him in an equally ebullient mood. She told Jack what time they had agreed on and they made their arrangements.

"Ok, I want to travel with Xav in his Porsche later," she decided. "You pick up Alex and we'll all meet at the Victor and go to the club later in both cars. Oh Jack, I'm so happy, it went really well. He's even going to let me go shopping with him!"

Jack never mentioned that it had not gone quite so smoothly with Alex, but he felt confident that he would be able to fix it.

***

Alex in the meantime had started to recover from that morning-after feeling. She had spent the afternoon relaxing in the sun with a good book and felt decidedly better. She would have liked to phone Xavier but had not thought to ask for his number. Besides it was best not to seem too desperate, he must be sick of being chased by women. Perhaps she would casually drop in over the next day or two, she had the perfect excuse to collect the shoes she had left there.

She tried not to dwell on him, but she could not believe she'd behaved so immaturely and literally passed out in front of him. It was just too embarrassing; she hoped he would put it all down to too much alcohol and sunshine. He hadn't seemed bothered in the slightest by the episode, but then he had done nothing wrong and behaved like a perfect gentleman. She put it out of mind, determined to deny the heat of her feelings and unexpected passion.

As for Jack, well he was just like an over-enthusiastic puppy, buying the picture for her was a very sweet thing to do. If she hadn't been so confused and shocked by his appearance in her kitchen, she wouldn't have been so ungracious. Next time she saw him she would put that right.

She had been upset at first by Jack's comment about Elaine and Xavier, but she rationalised that it was not her place to be jealous. After all, she hardly knew any of them; she couldn't really blame Elaine for being young and excited by a celebrity, especially after the way she'd behaved.

***

Elaine on the other hand was flying. She dropped in on her sister Sophie, who was feeding her two little girls. Elaine had rushed into the kitchen, flushed and excited.

"You won't believe who's got a date with Xavier de

Verre tonight! Me, me, me!" she shouted.

"No way!" Sophie exclaimed. "I don't believe you."

Captain Charles Dubois, their older brother and the chief of the local gendarmerie, was sitting in Sophie's kitchen. The way Elaine was dancing around it was clear that something earth-shattering had occurred. He watched this display with obvious disapproval.

"You are both idiots," he announced, turning directly to Elaine. "You will be used and thrown away like some silly tramp. What can a man like that, rich and famous, find interesting about you? Apart from the obvious?"

"Oh Charles," Sophie pleaded. "Don't be like that, can't you see how happy she is? You can't blame her, he's gorgeous."

"He's just some rich boy who has used his family to get on. People like you just reinforce his privileged position. I'd like to see how he would have done if he'd come from an honest, hard-working family, instead of that corrupt father and vacuous tart of a mother."

"You are just jealous, Charles!" Elaine cried, refusing to let him crush her dreams. "Jealous because you are a boring man, with no life and no future, stuck in this nothing town."

"You shut up," he shouted back, red-faced. Even

though he was only ten years older than Elaine, he seemed more like their parents every day.

"Just try not to make a fool of yourself and this family, that's all I'm asking. Some of us have reputations to consider, have some respect for that at least."

"I'm going Sophie, I can't listen to him. I'll call you tomorrow and let you know how it goes."

Elaine hugged her goodbye and then left, slamming the door as loudly as she could on the way out.

"Charles, she's young," Sophie reasoned. "Don't always be so tough on her, isn't life hard enough?"

"Mark my words Sophie, no good will come of this," Charles insisted. "She should grow up and you should stop encouraging her. You were married by the time you were her age, not running around like a little whore, fantasising about some rich celebrity coming to her rescue. She needs to get her head out of the clouds."

"What's this?" They both turned to see Sophie's husband, Jacques, standing in the doorway bashing the rich earth off his boots.

"Nothing," said Sophie, glaring at her brother.

Jacques could sense the tension and knew better than to interfere between his wife and her brother.

He was a large man, tall and quiet, who preferred to be working outside. He never complained about the back-breaking labour on the farm and had been quite happily married to Sophie for seven years. She also worked hard every day to provide a loving and productive life for her family. Elaine was the only one who was restless and unsettled.

Chapter 8

On different sides of Lassay, Xavier, Elaine and Jack were all getting ready for a night out. The missing link was Alex, who was engrossed in a book that she had bought some time ago and never got round to reading, still lounging in tracksuit bottoms and a t-shirt.

Jack felt confident that when he dropped by her house, he could persuade Alex to join them. He had not forgotten the earlier episode but this was different. There was something between them, he was certain. He had to get there early enough to give her time to get dressed and ready to look beautiful for him. Then he would drive her to the Victor for 9.00pm, ensuring that she would be dependent on him for a lift home later.

Elaine was taking particular care; she was going to wow Xav. She anticipated tonight would be very special indeed. She had carefully selected a skin-tight black dress, bought especially for such an occasion. The off-the-shoulder cut showed off her petite, curvy figure to perfection, leaving little to the imagination. Elaine knew she looked sultry and sexy and made her face up dramatically. She wanted to be drop-dead gorgeous and have all eyes upon her.

Xavier was lost in the beauty of his garden, admiring the evening sunshine and the variety of plants, rare climbing roses and early clematis blooming. He was wearing a casual, pale linen jacket but was excited at the thought of seeing Alex again. It would be good to keep it in a social setting, they could all speak English together instead of French. He could use a change of pace and a rare night out. He might even have fun and enjoy it, certainly Alex could make that happen if anyone could.

Jack decided his more dashing Armani jacket was needed to create the right impression. He had a wardrobe full of good clothes, gifts from previous lovers. He left it until 8.00pm to call on Alex, and was whistling to himself as he pulled down the driveway to her parents' farmhouse.

Alex had locked the door, but she reluctantly answered it when she heard Jack calling her name. She still wanted to pay for the picture he had brought her earlier and smooth over any ruffled feelings. She was not impressed when she found out Jack's real reason for stopping by.

"Come on Alex, we really want you to come along. You'll have a great time, we are going to the Victor and then on to La Pellu," he said, as if that meant something to her. She hardly came to rural France to go clubbing.

"You're on holiday. Relax, let your hair down. Xavier will be there," he tempted, although he was certain his charms would win her in the long run, Xavier would be busy with Elaine.

Yet no amount of gentle or firm persuasion would budge her resolve to keep her own company. Alex was fed up with being pushed into uncomfortable situations and she just wanted to be alone. She literally had to order Jack to leave again.

"Enough," she insisted. "I am not feeling well. I am staying home and it is time for you to leave. Now."

"Ok, I hear you," Jack responded eventually.

It was several moments of uncomfortable silence, before he finally got up and left for the second time that day. God, when would she learn?

***

Jack felt annoyed, but it was alright. He would make his peace with it. He was used to women who knew their own minds and he enjoyed it; he wasn't going to let her refusal bother him. Besides he had chosen the venue and he knew plenty of people there. He would have an excellent night with or without her. He wished he had some cocaine like his London days. He wondered if Xavier were into that sort of thing, although he seemed a bit square but he'd soon find out.

They all met in the Victor just after 9.00pm as planned. Jack ordered a bottle of wine and complimented Elaine on her appearance. Xavier seemed a little distracted, waiting for Alex to appear. Elaine was radiant as she chatted and laughed. She made her two male escorts relax as she flirted with them both, engaging with Xavier as much as she could.

Shortly before 11.00pm, with no sign of Alex, Xavier finally asked Jack if he had her number. Jack lied and said that he didn't, but she knew where they were going and presumably would turn up when she was ready. By now Elaine and Xavier were slightly drunk, unlike Jack who had poured for himself only the smallest servings of wine.

Jack had been watching Xavier carefully, he could tell that he hadn't come along because of Elaine. He liked that secret knowledge, it made him feel powerful. That feeling only increased when he managed to persuade Xavier to leave his Porsche in Lassay and let them all travel on to the next venue in his car. Looking back over that night, in the days to come, Xavier could not understand why he had let himself drink enough wine to agree.

They poured out of the Victor and Jack drove them through the dark countryside to the next venue. Xavier asked whether the gendarmerie would be out, but Jack, now in very high spirits, declared that he knew all the *'routes d'alcoolique'*, meaning the unpatrolled back roads, and it would be no problem.

La Pellu was packed despite the shabby interior. Clearly the clientele came for the pumping music and cheap drinks not the décor. Jack waved them all in and was immediately greeted on all sides by people he knew. The music throbbed and Elaine moved towards the dance floor and started bobbing and swaying to the sounds.

"Come on Xav, dance with me," she called over the din.

"Elaine, I don't dance." This was definitely not his scene.

"I'll dance with you, *chérie*."

Jack grabbed her hand and the two of them took to the dance floor, wildly grinding together in provocative motion. Xavier could see that they knew each other better than they had previously let on.

Xavier searched La Pellu for Alex, going back and forth checking faces. Eventually he settled in one of the booths, but still kept looking for her. Elaine left the dance floor and planted herself next to him. He felt edgy, she started running her hand up and down his arm. He became irritated by her constantly pawing at him.

Jack went past them on his way to the bathroom, stopping a few times to talk to friends before he disappeared amongst the crowd. Elaine took the opportunity to focus completely on Xavier.

“I have to work for the rest of the week, Xav,” she shouted over the noise. “But I can try to take Friday off if you want to go and look in Laval for some things for your house?”

Only his closest friends called him ‘Xav’. He didn’t class Elaine in that category and it annoyed him to hear her using the shortened version of his name. He was saved from having to answer her question by Jack returning, carrying a bottle of vodka for the table.

“Shots!” he declared.

Another couple Xavier didn’t know were tagging along behind him. They joined the party and the atmosphere heightened as they all tossed back neat shots.

Xavier felt slightly queasy because of the vodka he had struggled down, on top of the thumping base that was getting to him. He felt trapped without his car, totally stuck by his own stupid actions. He shouldn’t be here, it served him right. He estimated that they had driven at least ten or more kilometres from Lassay, and it was a long way to walk in unfamiliar territory.

Another bottle of vodka had been ordered and Jack and Elaine disappeared off to dance again. Xavier brooded and decided to fortify himself with another shot, one for the road. This wouldn't have been right, even if Alex had come along, he couldn't imagine her enjoying this. It certainly wasn't how he had anticipated their next meeting after the beautiful night they'd spent together.

Jack and Elaine returned sweating and out of breath, then poured more shots. Elaine was falling about on her heels, before attempting to sit on Xavier's lap so he moved along the booth to give her space. She slid even closer, rubbing herself against him making it clear what she expected from the rest of the night.

"Xav, let's get out of here. I want you so badly to fuck me," she boldly looked up into his eyes, with parted red lips and liquid green eyes, filled with lust.

That was it. No matter what it would cost him in blistered feet, he was leaving. Xavier stood up, made an excuse to get away and instead of going to the bathroom, he walked straight out of the front of the club and into the night.

Xavier knew he could walk it and was not bothered by the challenge. If he headed south-west, he would eventually find his way towards Lassay. He felt most at home in the countryside and the darkness did not trouble him. He was grateful that years of working outside in nature had left him with a built-in compass.

As he breathed in the cool, fresh night air, he felt an overwhelming drunkenness and had to sit on the side of the road for what seemed like ages to get his body back under control. He decided to lay and look at the stars for as long as it took.

***

Elaine and Jack were grinding to the latest tunes on the dance floor, when it struck Elaine that Xavier was taking a long time. They found their booth empty.

“Jack, where’s Xav?” she shouted above the sounds.

“I don’t know. Go and get another drink and I’ll check it out,” he promised. She headed to look for him at the bar.

Jack couldn’t find Xavier anywhere. When he spoke to his friend Annie at reception, she told him that Xavier had left about twenty minutes before. Jack returned to the bar and told Elaine, who was extremely upset.

“Why?” she screeched. “Why would he just walk off and say nothing? What’s wrong with the guy? Do you think he was sick?”

“I don’t know Elaine. Don’t worry about it, just

enjoy yourself. He's certainly got a long walk home," he was obviously amused by that, take the big shot television star down a peg or two.

Elaine was not so easily pacified. She felt the tears beginning, she couldn't believe it! Nobody rejected her advances; it had never happened before and she wasn't going to let the biggest prize of her life walk out on her without even saying goodbye. No way, she was going after him. She went back to the table to collect her bag.

"Don't act crazy, Elaine," Jack followed her. "Leave the guy, he's not worth it. What are you going to achieve chasing after him in the darkness, especially wearing those shoes?"

Jack tried to reason and get some sense into her but Elaine wasn't listening. She was drunk and emotional, tears starting to fall in humiliated rivers down her cheeks.

"Look, give me five minutes. I have to catch up with Christian over there, then I'll be back and take you home, ok?"

When Jack returned from his conversation, she was gone.

***

The man gently manoeuvred her off the country road and into the dark wooded copse. Elaine fell against his muscled chest, sobbing as he held her firmly in strong arms. She dropped to her knees and drunkenly fumbled to undo his trousers and release him into her open, waiting red lips. She tried to take as much of his huge cock into her mouth as possible and he wound his fingers through her thick dark hair, pushing himself further down her throat, making her gag. She tried to pull away but he wouldn't let her, thrusting into her mouth.

In one move he pulled her to her feet and pushed her hard against the trunk of a large oak, the bark cutting into her back. He lifted her off the ground, pressing her up against the tree as she wrapped her legs around him. Pulling her tiny dress up above her hips and ripping off the lacy thong, he filled her body with his. She moaned at the feel of him inside her and clung to him as he pushed harder and harder into her. In a frantic coupling of unleashed passion, crying out involuntarily at the strength of her explosion, she came to a shuddering climax, immediately spent and exhausted.

He threw her limp body to the ground; he wasn't finished with her. Rolling her onto her back, he pushed her legs forcefully over her head and started to pump her open, exposed body like a man possessed. Suddenly, drunken desire was replaced by fear.

"Please stop!" she begged.

His response was to force her over onto her knees like a dog, pushing even deeper into her from behind. He was clutching and bruising her hips with vice-like fingers that pulled her back and forwards upon him. Elaine desperately tried to get away, crying and begging him to let her go, but he never responded. He was totally silent apart from the grunting sounds that came out of his mouth with each violent thrust.

She felt a searing pain as he brutally shoved his cock deep inside her anus. Now total panic took over, she tried to fight him but he pushed her face into the ground, suffocating her and silencing her screams as she struggled to breathe. Still he carried on, torturing her body.

'Please God, help me, save me,' was like a mantra endlessly repeated in her head, trying to numb the agony. Gradually darkness overwhelmed her and detached her screaming mind from her body and the fatal onslaught. As her face choked on the earth, she finally knew no more.

Chapter 9

Xavier awoke the next day to the sound of the telephone ringing. He tried to lift his head from the pillow but was forced back by the thudding, dull pain of his hangover. Gingerly he swung his legs over the side of the bed and tried to sit up. He couldn't think through the fog that had replaced his normally sharp mind, but when his feet touched the ground he winced in pain. It was an immediate reminder of the marathon walk home from the club last night.

He tried to gather up his dirty clothes from the floor, but the effort of bending over made him feel sick. The phone started ringing again and he snatched it up quickly to stop the noise. It was his agent, Jean-Louis, calling from Paris.

"Where have you been for Christ's sake? I've been trying to call you. The people from Paramount Television have arrived. I've scheduled a meeting for 5.00pm."

Xavier groaned audibly.

"This is important, Xavier," the agent went on

emphatically. "We can't miss this opportunity."

"Ok, calm down. What's the time?" asked Xavier, trying to pull himself together.

"You have four hours to make it, so get moving. Now," demanded Jean-Louis, hanging up the phone.

Already 1.00pm, my God, thought Xavier to himself. As quickly as humanly possible he showered and put on clean, presentable clothes. He fortified himself with two espressos, then locked his house and jumped into his Porsche and headed for Paris.

***

Jack was in excellent form. He busied himself tidying the reception area of the hotel, placing the brochures advertising local tourist attractions and upcoming events into piles on the rack. He hummed one of the tunes from the club last night that had got stuck in his head and every now and then broke into a little dance. He heard the front door open and turned to see a slightly built, middle-aged blonde standing nervously in the doorway.

"Sorry to bother you." The woman apologised before she'd even said anything and Jack waited expectantly.

"My name is Jayne Slater," she went on. "A friend

told me that you were English, so I thought that maybe you could help me."

"Hi Jayne," said Jack, flashing his brilliant smile and immediately putting her at ease. "What can I do for you?"

"Well, I'm looking for some work," she started hesitantly. "It doesn't matter what. I don't speak French, so maybe cleaning or something like that?"

"This is your lucky day, Jayne. I have twelve bedrooms to clean, and to be honest, it's the last thing I want to do today. When can you start?" Jack could not believe his good fortune.

"Right away," said Jayne gratefully.

"Excellent!" he replied. "Let's have a coffee and I'll go through it with you. It's not rocket science so I'm sure you'll be just fine." Jack smiled winningly again as he came around the counter to shake her little hand with his large strong one, thoroughly pleased with his new staff member.

They spent the next hour drinking coffee whilst Jayne told Jack her story and he listened sympathetically. He'd heard the same sort of tale many times before; Brits had been arriving in this part of France for years searching for a new life. They usually came with the money from the sale of a house in the UK, bought up a wreck or shell of a farmhouse somewhere and attempted to live the good life on dreams and dwindling capital.

Renovations were enormously expensive, walls crumbled and fell and had to be re-built; what seemed like an achievable project, for the naïve and those without relevant experience, suitable skills or even basic French, soon turned into a living hell. The majority of them were escaping inner-city lives and very few were equipped to survive the harsh reality of country living.

Work was hard to come by, so Jayne's husband Tom had been forced to return to his old job as a delivery man in Manchester to earn some money for them to live on, leaving Jayne stranded in a foreign country where she neither understood the language, nor the reason for them being there anymore.

It was hard being alone all the time. She'd tried to keep up with the vegetable plot and care for the animals. She had stupidly named them after Disney characters so was not able to kill and eat them as planned. Little Thumper was never going to be on her dinner table or fill her empty stomach.

Jayne felt embarrassed as she explained to Jack that Tom hadn't been home for six weeks now. She wasn't sure how much longer she could hold out with no money. Jayne kept to herself her fear that Tom had found a new relationship with the woman he rented a room from and was never coming back.

Jack listened patiently feeling sorry for her, then took out his wallet.

"Listen, take these forty euros now," he held out the notes.

"Oh, no I couldn't," said Jayne, still reaching out to accept the money from his outstretched hand. "I haven't done anything yet."

"Don't worry, by the time you've finished this lot you will have earnt it," he promised.

Jayne smiled at him, genuinely relieved and her face relaxed. Jack noticed for the first time that she was actually quite attractive. Her long ash-blonde hair was tied back in a tight ponytail but looked natural and her eyes were pale blue. Her complexion was clear and fresh and didn't give away her thirty-eight years.

Jack could see that she would scrub up well if she made the effort. Jayne's figure was still slim from endless hours of toil on her land, unlike her husband Tom, whose girth had increased over the years in proportion to their diminishing sex-life.

Jack showed Jayne around Le Petit Château, the small hotel named after the castle, and explained what he wanted her to do during the brief tour of the rooms.

"It will only be a couple of days a week for now

Jayne, but in July the hotel has a lot of bookings so I should think I'll need you every day then," he showed her to the cleaning cupboard.

Jayne left the hotel later that day having scrubbed and polished as though her very life depended on it. She felt better than she had in ages, invigorated by the sudden change in her fortune. Jack was a godsend and his amazing good looks had not escaped her attention either, although she hadn't let her eyes linger on his strong, muscular frame or handsome face for too long, for fear that her blushing cheeks would give her away.

Jack waited for Jayne to leave before immediately jumping into his car and speeding off up the road towards Alex's parents' farmhouse. As he left the village, he passed Xavier's closed gates and the house looked as dead as a mausoleum. He briefly wondered how the poor bastard had managed on his long walk last night and gave a little chuckle at the thought.

Alex looked stunning as he pulled into the drive and he could not take his eyes off her. She was laying in the garden wearing the smallest pink bikini revealing all of her perfectly bronzed, glamour model body. She tried to cover herself with a matching filmy sarong as she saw Jack approaching, but not before he had feasted himself on the image. He had not been expecting such killer curves.

"Hi," he said, producing a chilled bottle of champagne from behind his back and holding it up for her to see.

"Stay where you are, I'll get the glasses," he announced, as he walked into the house in his familiar way and opened a few cupboards, before finding two flutes and returning to the terrace.

As Jack popped the cork and filled the glasses, handing one to Alex, she found it hard not to warm to his sunny disposition even if he was the most annoying person.

"To the most beautiful woman in the world," he toasted.

"Really Jack, will you ever get used to the idea of being invited? Or even calling before you turn up?" she said, unable to stop herself from smiling.

"Never!" he replied. "You don't have to cover up on my behalf, I'm already smitten. Even if I live to be a hundred, the vision of you laying there will always be my most perfect moment."

"You sir, are a scoundrel and a rogue," she responded playfully. The champagne had gone straight to her head.

"I'll drink to that! And long may we rule the earth," Jack drained his glass.

They sat and enjoyed the afternoon sunshine and

continued with the playful banter.

"Just call me Sir Galahad today," he said, then Jack told her about Jayne.

"That poor woman." Alex was immediately sympathetic to her plight. "Why do they put themselves in that position? It's crazy."

"They don't know," said Jack. "There's a saying that they leave their brains on the ferry on the way here. I suspect they just visit one year during the summer holiday and fall for the place. They love the tranquillity, but people don't think about the consequences of actually living and working out here."

Alex nodded, she knew how difficult it had been for her parents over the years getting work done on the house and trying to be understood. Jack carried on his lecture.

"There are different rules and more importantly, a different language to master. You can't realistically expect to live in France if you don't speak French. It's ok for the retired ones, they have a whole ex-pat community here and socialise amongst themselves. Unless you're on a pension, sooner or later you will have to go to work and you need to be able to communicate."

Alex had enough champagne in her to interrupt him and change the subject to what she was really interested in.

"How did it go last night?"

She wanted details about Xavier and Elaine, but Jack wasn't giving anything away.

"Yeah great. We had a really good night. We got totally smashed, but hey, that was the reason for going." He looked pleased with himself. "You should have come along Alex, you would have enjoyed it."

Alex seriously doubted that. She'd had enough to drink the other night and made a fool of herself. No more carrying on like this; but even as she thought it, she found herself wondering if she had a bottle of rose wine in the fridge. No wonder so many of the Brits who moved to France started drinking from lunch-time onwards. If she lived out here, she would end up an alcoholic.

"No, I'm glad I stayed home. I came here to get away from stress and have no need for any excitement. I will leave you youngsters to it," she joked, wondering how to pry for more information without revealing her intentions.

"Yes mum," replied Jack, giving her his most cheeky, boyish grin. "So, what's wrong with your ex, Alex? How could he let a babe like you get away?"

"I don't really want to talk about John," she frowned, but before long found herself pouring out all the years of frustration and disappointment, whilst Jack did what he did best, listen and absorb her pain.

Chapter 10

By Monday afternoon, Sophie was certain something was wrong with her sister. It was normal for the young people to be out late on any given night of the week, they stayed over at friends' houses all the time. It was not normal for Elaine to be unreachable, with no response from her phone which went straight to voicemail. She was always on her mobile, it felt unnatural not to be able to get hold of her.

Their mother had phoned during the morning to find out if Elaine had stayed with her, so Sophie knew she had not been home last night. Madame Lacroix from the hairdressers had also telephoned the Dubois farm, when Elaine hadn't showed up for work that morning.

Madame Dubois was worried but Elaine's father was silent as usual, neither surprised nor interested in her failing to come home or turn up at work. He was fed up with his wayward daughter, thinking this behaviour typical of his spoilt youngest child. He would prefer to see her find a nice village boy and settle down, but he wasn't holding his breath and she was still crashing around his house for the time being. Would he ever get any peace?

Sophie had phoned all the close friends of Elaine she could think of, but none of them had seen her. She didn't know the telephone number for Xavier de Verre or she would have called him too. The gnawing sense of unease kept growing all day, until she couldn't leave it any longer. With dread she picked up the phone to call her brother Charles.

"Elaine is missing," she faltered.

"Stop it, Sophie," Charles was annoyed. "I'm sure she's shacked up with that playboy, de Verre. I'm not going to lower myself to go round there and find them in bed together. She'll come crawling home when he chucks her out."

"Please Charles," she insisted. "I know she would have phoned me by now if she was ok."

"Why? Do you think she cares how we feel? Do you think she is the slightest bit concerned for her family? I am the chief of the gendarmerie and I have a reputation to uphold. Did she consider that before she dropped her knickers for that charlatan?" He paused for breath, daring his sister to reply, before he carried on. "It's all about her Sophie, it always is. She doesn't think about how her actions affect us!"

Sophie could not listen to another word and

cut him off, dropping her head into her hands in frustration. Please phone Elaine, she prayed, instinctively crossing herself. What on earth had happened to her sister? She knew that if Elaine's plans had come to fruition and she had scored with the fantastic Xavier, she would have been on the phone by now telling Sophie all about it. Something was not right, she could feel it.

***

Xavier made it to the Hôtel George V in the super-chic Parisian quarter of Saint-Germain-des-Près, with fifteen minutes to spare before the meeting with the Paramount Television executives. Jean-Louis was pacing the luxurious black and white marble floor tiles of the hotel lobby, anxiously looking around and glancing at his watch. As Xavier entered the foyer, the agent rushed up to him theatrically.

"What has happened to you? You look terrible, Xavier," he complained, although heads turned as they strode through the lobby.

"Quick, I've got to get a coffee. Do you have the paperwork, Jean-Louis?" Xavier ignored the jibe.

"Yes, of course, I've been working. Working on your behalf, I might add," the agent sniffed.

"Get me a coffee, I'll be with you in two minutes."

Xavier rushed to the bathroom where he splashed

his face with cold water, ran his fingers through his thick dark hair and did his level best to brush up for a meeting he knew he was in no shape to handle. He joined Jean-Louis in the coffee shop feeling marginally better. The executives had seen his volume of work, he would just have to coast his way through and play it cool.

The meeting went much better than Xavier had expected, due mainly to the fact that two of the three American executives were women. These ladies had indeed watched some of the previous episodes of *Le Monde Naturel* and seen what Xavier's tanned body looked like stripped off.

His French accent completed the fantasy and his spoken English was excellent and easily understood. Xavier held himself together admirably, he was passionate and articulate about his work. The meeting was a success; a deal was signed and a fee structure agreed in principle for all three series.

Xavier breathed a sigh of relief and joined Jean-Louis in the hotel bar for a celebratory glass of champagne.

"Congratulations," said Jean-Louis, raising his glass. "It looks like you are going to be an international star. You deserve this Xavier, you've worked long and hard to achieve this accolade. Well done and good luck to you! *Santé*!"

"*Santé*," Xavier replied, clinking glasses and toasting his health in return.

"And obviously good fortune to me, that was a tidy sum we've just signed for. Tonight, I'm a very happy agent." Jean-Louis was fulfilled.

For the first time that day, Xavier started to relax. It really was a wonderful achievement and he would have liked to celebrate, but he couldn't cope with another night of drinking. Nor would he manage the long drive back to Lassay this evening. He would go back to his studio in the fashionable Boulevard Saint-Michel and recharge his batteries.

He couldn't help thinking about Alex, he wanted to share the good news with her. He felt the instinct to get to know her better, to protect her, to keep her safe from the world. He couldn't wait to feel her in his arms again, savour the sweet smell of her body close to his. He would put the other night behind him and proceed with careful control. No more messing around, he knew what he wanted and would do anything to get it.

***

Jayne had treated herself to a box of cheap wine with some of her forty euros. She knew she shouldn't have, but she had worked hard and felt like she deserved it. She relaxed in the deckchair outside the door to her dilapidated, half-finished kitchen with a glass of red wine in her hand.

Maybe things were looking up after all, she thought, as she reflected on her day, grateful for the change in her situation. Reluctantly, she made the call to her husband Tom, but it went straight to voicemail again so she left a brief message.

It was a warm June evening and she was grateful for the peace. The garden was well-tended and the privacy was bliss, even if sometimes lonely. Although she preferred being alone to being desperate, broke and unable to cover her living expenses.

It was exactly a night like this two years ago that her and Tom had celebrated the purchase of their house. Up until now, she had kept secret the great deal of regret she had regarding that decision. This had been the most difficult few years of her life and now Tom was no longer here to even pretend to share the burden.

This evening she felt different for the first time in a long time, surprisingly intoxicated and warmed from within. She wasn't sure if it was the effect of the wine, or the thoughts that kept popping into her head about the gorgeous Jack Winter.

She let her hand wander aimlessly across her breast and gently started pinching her nipple until she could feel it harden. She couldn't stop herself from imagining what he would feel like. He was big, would he be big all over? Stop, Jayne! she chided herself.

She continued to gently massage her breasts and then moved her hand lower, until she was rhythmically pressing the spot her husband never quite found. Her breathing quickened as she kept up the fast rubbing until she exploded into an exquisite orgasm, all the time imagining the face and strong body of Jack hovering above her.

Less than two kilometres from where Jayne Slater luxuriated in the afterglow of her orgasm, the horribly, obscenely mangled body of Elaine Dubois lay in the dark copse, as tiny creatures invaded every crevasse of her lifeless body. Unless she was discovered soon, she would keep rotting in this heat and attract more insects and wildlife. Her sister Sophie worried, but the rest of her family felt nothing but annoyed and inconvenienced.

Chapter 11

Tuesday arrived and there was still no sign of Elaine and nobody had heard from her. Sophie's nagging had persuaded her brother Charles Dubois, as chief of the local gendarmerie, to pay a visit to Xavier de Verre. Everyone in town knew he had bought the English woman's house and decided to play the big man, lord of the manor. He knew the type alright and was not impressed by his celebrity status or famous family.

Charles pulled up outside in his official vehicle. He realised the front gates were closed but not locked, and so he opened them and walked up to the front of the house. He noted that no car was in the driveway. He knocked a few times on the door, but it was evident that nobody was home. He tried looking around the back, peering in through the un-shuttered windows for any sign of life.

What he saw only added to his sense of injustice. How the other half live, he thought to himself bitterly. He couldn't keep from feeling jealous as he regarded the luxury of the interior. He could only dream of owning such a house on his wages.

Like so many others, he would only experience a glimpse of such life on television.

He wondered whether de Verre was truly foolish enough to have taken his troublesome little sister to Paris. Well good luck to him; hopefully she'd stay there, he was sure they deserved each other. It was just like Elaine to take off without even the courtesy of saying goodbye, leaving behind her family to worry about her whereabouts.

As far as he was concerned, he had done his duty. The fact that he had visited would be enough to pacify Sophie and his mother. He was about to leave, when he realised he had left the gates open, as a UK registered car eased into the driveway. Even Charles pulled himself up a little taller when Alex emerged from the car.

"*Bonjour mademoiselle.*"

"*Bonjour monsieur*," Alex faltered. She had not been expecting the gendarmerie. "I'm afraid I don't speak French."

"That is not a problem mademoiselle, we are trained to speak English. These days, it has become necessary unfortunately," he added rudely. "What are you doing here?"

"I'm visiting my friend, but he doesn't appear to be home so I'll leave." She turned away from him to get back into her car.

"Not so quickly, mademoiselle," Charles stopped her. "I have a few questions if you don't mind."

"Of course not," Alex responded, although she felt decidedly uneasy. "Is Xavier ok? Has there been an accident?"

"Not that I know of. I believe Monsieur Xavier de Verre went out on Monday night with Mademoiselle Elaine Dubois. Do you know anything about this?" he decided to ask her outright.

"No, I'm sorry I don't," replied Alex. "What is the problem?"

"I am sure there is no problem, but neither of them has been seen since and it is causing the Dubois family some concern. Do you know Elaine?"

"We met a few times, she cut my hair when I first arrived last week. It was on Friday," Alex remembered. "Then I saw her again on the day of the street painting. I never went out on Sunday night with the others."

"The others?"

"Elaine, Xavier and Jack Winter."

Captain Dubois frowned at the mention of his name. This was clearly news to him and it was time to get some more information from the girl.

"*Excuse-moi mademoiselle*, I have neglected to ask for your name." Charles reached into his pocket for a small notebook and pencil.

"I'm Alexandra Taylor," she replied and he wrote it down.

"How do you know Xavier de Verre?" he continued.

"We met at the painting day. Last Saturday at the Victor pub."

She never considered not replying, she wanted to know what was going on. Had something happened to Xavier? Or was he just off with Elaine somewhere having the time of his life? Had he whisked another girl to Paris and just disappeared on her?

"Would you have Monsieur de Verre's private telephone number, Mademoiselle Taylor?" Charles pressed.

There was nobody to stop him questioning her, but as a very recent and casual acquaintance, she could not be expected to know much about either of them.

"I'm sorry, I can't help you with that," responded Alex.

Even if she had Xav's number, not only would she not give it to this pompous prick, but she'd throw it away as soon as she could. In fact, she'd burn it!

How could she have been so taken in by him? It was definitely a combination of booze and heat she reasoned, but all that lust and pointless speculation for nothing. A silly girl's daydreams, an indulgent fantasy, when prince charming had already moved on to the next.

Charles Dubois was not easily fooled. He could only guess at the internal dialogue going on in her mind, but he could see that she was put out by the information that she had received. Another stupid woman, falling all over de Verre, he mused. He would remember that, always good to sniff out any weakness or reason to lie.

"If you don't mind, I have some shopping to do," Alex said, excusing herself. She couldn't wait to get away.

"If you see either Elaine Dubois or Xavier de Verre, would you please tell them to call the Lassay gendarmerie and ask to speak to the chief," he dismissed her, nodding towards her car.

Charles deliberately omitted to give his name, as this was not yet any kind of formal investigation. The girl was clearly clueless but one thing was for certain, Xavier de Verre was not in his house in Lassay.

***

Alex drove into town feeling humiliated and angry

with herself. She bought the few provisions she needed and added two bottles of wine for good measure. She felt like numbing her over-active imagination and was already thoroughly worked up. She couldn't get Jack's words out of her head, about Elaine always getting her man. Well may they both rot in French hell!

She was just getting back into her car when she spotted Jack coming towards her smiling. She really didn't want to see him but it was too late to drive off.

"Hey, Alex," he called to her.

As soon as he saw her dark expression, he knew something was up. He had a nose for vulnerability.

"Are you ok, babe?" he asked solicitously.

"Sure, fine," she lied.

"You don't look fine, if it's not too rude to say it. You look about ready to bite someone's head off. What's wrong?"

"Oh Jack, it's not you. I've just heard that Xavier and Elaine are missing," she explained. "Do you know what happened to them? Did you see them leave together on Sunday when you went out?"

"I'm sorry Alex, I don't remember," Jack answered evasively. "They left the club before me, and I was kind of drunk. I didn't really take much notice." He took a moment to consider carefully how best to take advantage of this unexpected opportunity.

"Look, I've got to get back to the hotel," he said, but thinking quickly, allowing time for her to get stuck into those clinking bottles, he decided to go for it. "I'll pop round later, just to make sure you're ok."

"No, Jack, it's not necessary," Alex insisted. "I'm perfectly fine, really I am."

"Well, I'll ask around and see what I can find out. Somebody must know something," he offered.

He grabbed her close and gave her a kiss on each cheek.

"Later gorgeous," he added into her hair, but she was oblivious.

Alex did not want to see anyone, now or later. She went home and pulled the cork on the first bottle, quickly downed the glass of merlot and poured another. France was proving to be a big mistake, and to think she'd come here to get away from her problems.

Why hadn't she just stuck to the house as she had intended? She could have spent her time sleeping and reading, eating wonderful food and wine, having a lovely relaxing break. That at least would have been pleasant, safe, trouble-free; but no, she had to go out, make life difficult for herself, get into complications and now look what had happened.

She just couldn't stop thinking about Elaine and Xavier. She was enraged at how upset she was and how much she cared. They were probably in Paris, Elaine told her it was her dream to go there. She must have been a good lay for him to take her away with him. They could be in bed right now, her mind continued to rampage summoning unwanted images of him and the French girl to torment her, locked together in passion.

She paced up and down the kitchen, drinking her wine and making desperate plans. She would head home, cut her trip short, better to be at work busy. At least she could go back to the office and get on with her real life. She'd avoid all possible relationships with any man ever again!

It was getting dark and she wondered where the day had gone since her brush with the gendarmerie. Alex was just opening her second bottle and feeling better now she had decided on a plan of action, when she heard a tapping at the front door and could not remember if she had locked it. As she was considering whether she wanted to answer, Jack's blonde head peeked around the kitchen door.

"Alex, are you there? Can I come in?"

Jack seemed unusually hesitant, normally he just walked in and made himself at home. She had almost got used to his familiar way, veering between over-friendly and inappropriate, but just barely staying on the right side. She wasn't sure how she felt about him barging in again.

"I see you're making good headway," he said, pointing to the bottle. "Lucky I bought my own."

Unpacking his shopping bag, he put two more bottles of red wine onto the kitchen table. Alex was yet to say anything, as if she was trying to make a decision.

"Would you prefer it if I went?" he offered.

"No Jack, stay," she made up her mind. "You seem to be the only person I can talk to right now."

"You know I only want to be your friend, Alex. I can tell you are upset about Elaine and Xavier," he stated the obvious, fetching himself a wine glass, then taking a seat across from her at the table.

"I tried to warn you, they're different from us the French. Fidelity is not their strong point."

"He seemed so nice, Jack. I'm so stupid," she confessed, on the edge of tears. "I thought he really liked me."

Jack didn't know what she was talking about, but the alcohol had loosened her tongue and it all came tumbling out. She told him about the night she had accidentally stayed at Xavier's house.

She was sitting at the table pouring one glass of wine after another, while she described her humiliation, big tears rolling down her cheeks.

He didn't try to stop her, just wondered if he'd need to go out for more supplies. No, he reckoned she would pass out if she didn't stop soon. He considered when would be the perfect moment to make his move, whether she was at just the right pitch of drunkenness and need.

Alex was getting herself progressively more upset and still off on her rant. She was filled with sorrow and self-pity for her miserable life.

"Would you like a broad shoulder to do that crying on?"

Jack went round to her side of the table. He very carefully stood her up and drew her to him in an embrace.

"There, there baby," he soothed as he rubbed her back and hair. "Let it all out, you'll feel much better afterwards. You just need some time to heal. I know, I understand."

Alex wasn't quite sure how the friendly cuddle turned into a kiss, but she didn't resist. She had little willpower or resolve left; the crying and the booze had gradually worn her out. She was fragile from releasing the emotional burden of her secret on to another party. She liked being close to him.

Jack's tender kisses made her feel warm and wanted. She swayed in his arms as his lips left her mouth and slowly went down her face to her neck. She instinctively flung her head back so that he could continue, craving more, revelling in the intimacy.

Jack wasn't drunk, he was determined to savour every sweet moment. This is what he'd wanted since he first set eyes on her in town. With one arm circling her tiny waist and holding her up, he dropped his head until he was kissing her shoulder, her chest. He gently stroked her beautiful bust through the fabric of her vest, until he'd released her straps and revealed the naked flesh his hand had been gently caressing.

He took her erect nipple into his mouth, first one and then the other, as he pulled the top down around her waist and pressed his face between her breasts. His voice was husky with passion as he moaned her name, steering her towards the stairs, whispering his desires to her, never letting go. She pointed to her bedroom, assenting all the way, wanting this to happen. It had been a long time since she had felt this kind of drunken abandon.

Jack lowered her down onto the bed, fumbling for the lamp so he could see her. He felt like a conquering king about to claim his rightful prize. God she was beautiful, she was his now, his queen. She was what he deserved, none of the others could ever compare. He was going to show her what it felt like to be made love to by a real man.

Very slowly Jack peeled off what remained of her clothing until she was lying naked. He stood gazing at her whilst she sensuously stretched out her arms and legs in shameless invitation. She surrendered herself willingly to the warm mouth that kissed the length of her body, until he was between her legs, his strong hands firmly lifting her buttocks towards his face. His tongue reached inside her, she moaned and moved herself upwards for more, pressing against his face.

Gradually he removed his own clothes, no quick moves, until finally he was as naked as her. As he drew away for the first time, his face came level with hers and he looked into her eyes. He stared directly at her as he eased his swollen cock into the wet space his tongue had just left. He was so big, she gasped out loud as she felt the full length of him, but she was wet, open and willing.

“Beg for it,” he demanded.

“Please fuck me, Jack!” she cried.

Jack thrust the full length of his member into her hard, then withdrew and shoved again. He fell on top of her, pounding her body and thrilled by the heat of her response, joining him in his controlled rhythm as he found his pace, building faster and faster until she was crying out, digging her nails into his back as she clung to him, pushing her hips towards his with a matched intensity.

When they finally climaxed, it was together as one, wave after wave of delicious orgasm shuddering through their bodies as he pumped into her and filled her with his sperm. They lay together spent for a few moments, until he rolled her over on top of him, both of them laughing breathlessly at their unexpected, unleashed passion.

Chapter 12

When Alex awoke the next morning she was alone. She wondered if she had dreamed the previous night or if it had really happened. Had she just experienced the best sex of her life with Jack? Her head was still swimming, so she went straight to the bathroom and took a long shower.

Thank goodness she'd continued to take her contraceptive pill; she was horrified at the risk she had taken. How many lovers had he had recently? What if she caught something? The encounter with Jack had been amazing; but in the cold light of day, she wasn't sure that it would be sensible to repeat it.

Jack was born again; this was love, he was sure of it. He had gone into town to find a dozen red roses and was just returning with the items for the breakfast he'd planned. He couldn't wait to get back to Alex; he hoped she would still be in bed, as hungry for him as he was for her, wanting to continue where they had left off the night before.

Arriving back at the house, he was disappointed to find her up and dressed in an embroidery anglaise sundress, looking cool and clean, her hair still wet from the shower. He rushed into the kitchen with his arms full of roses, but the look on her face stopped him from pouring out what was in his heart. He recovered himself in a split second and tried to adopt the same casual air that she emanated.

“Roses for my queen,” he said in a lightly flirtatious way, offering them to her with a mock bow.

“Now, I insist on preparing you breakfast, just to say thank you for a wonderful night of passion.”

Jack tried to kiss her on the mouth, but she turned her face so that his lips landed on her cheek.

“I feel like a naughty child,” she said blushing.

“I'd rather have the wanton slut,” he mumbled under his breath and turned his back on her, busying himself with the breakfast preparation.

“Jack, are you disappointed?” Alex questioned, concerned by the shift in his sunny countenance.

“No, of course not,” he replied shortly.

Jack was much more than disappointed; he felt devastated, cheated and betrayed.

“You better get those flowers into water before they wilt.”

Alex tried to make light conversation about her

plans for the day, but had to admit that it was increasingly awkward and heavy-going. She was pleased when Jack left to return to work in the hotel, he was expecting clients to arrive that morning and had to get back.

It was yet another warm sunny day and Alex decided to spend it alone and finish her book. She would think later about changing her return ferry to an earlier date.

***

Jack slammed the door of the hotel behind him, went behind the desk and took a big swig out of the whiskey bottle he kept there. Fuck her, he thought, and that's what he should have done. Making love was over-rated, it would never replace a good fuck. Jack admired his reflection in the mirror behind the reception. What was Alex's problem?

He heard a sound in the kitchen and was alert and listening for movement, when he remembered that Jayne was due in that morning to clean and freshen up the rooms for the clients they were expecting. He opened the door and saw her kneeling on the floor, picking up broken pieces of something.

"Hi Jayne."

"I'm sorry, Jack, I dropped a cup," she explained, jumping up at the sound of his voice.

"Don't worry sweetheart," he said charmingly, amused by her obvious embarrassment at being caught.

"I'm glad to see you," he continued. "You've brightened up my day."

"Really?" said Jayne, a rush of confusing thoughts running through her brain. Her cheeks burned when one in particular settled, as she remembered her pleasuring herself the other night whilst fantasising about this man.

"Drop what you're doing and join me for a drink," he commanded. "I feel like the company of an attractive woman."

They went through to the reception and Jack poured her a shot of whiskey. Jayne didn't normally like whiskey but she never said a word, just took it from him and reluctantly sipped at the harsh liquid. Jack downed another two shots in quick succession. It's a bit early to be drinking like that, Jayne thought, he must be disturbed by something.

"Are you alright Jack?" she ventured tentatively.

"Yep, great. Why do you ask? Am I acting strange?"

"No, no, I didn't mean to be nosy. Sorry," she mumbled, looking down at the floor.

"Stop apologising, you're always saying sorry. Why

is that, Jayne?"

Leaning in towards her, he took her chin in his hand and stared straight at her.

"Is it because you're a naughty girl, by any chance?"

At that exact moment, the British couple they were expecting arrived struggling with a large suitcase. Jack smoothly booked them in, offering advice about local places of interest and helping the husband by effortlessly carrying the heavy bag upstairs for him.

Jayne finished her work and quickly left, flustered by Jack's words and his touch. It was like he knew what she'd been up to, he could smell it on her. He could sense she wanted him sexually, which in turn made her feel more excited. He definitely seemed to be coming on to her. Was it pathetic that she was keenly interested? This was the most attention she had received in months.

***

In Paris, Xavier had woken bright and early, refreshed and ready for the drive to Lassay. He was excited to return and get back to Alex. He wanted to see what came of this chance encounter, but he felt certain this woman could be important to him. She was unlike anyone he had known, so natural and graceful and entirely without artifice.

He had already been delayed by Jean-Louis'

insistence that they should take the American executives to dinner in Paris as a courtesy before they returned to Los Angeles, show them a few sights and impress them with their beautiful city.

Jean-Louis had booked Ducasse sur Seine, a floating restaurant from the world's most Michelin-starred chef that meandered gently along the river, whilst its clients enjoyed exquisite French haute cuisine and feasted their eyes on some of Paris' most famous attractions.

Xavier had recovered from his hangover and his dash to the capital. He was captivating and vibrant as he enthusiastically discussed his plans for the next series in his intense Gallic way. By the time they all parted, he had the normally hard-nosed executives charmed and eating out of his hand.

The evening had been an unmitigated success. Xavier had to acknowledge that making the extra effort for the Paramount executives had been a clever idea, and reminded himself to select a special gift for his agent, to say thank you for many years of solid advice and representation.

Now it was Wednesday, and he was finally about to leave a day later than planned, when he received a call from his imperious mother Yvette de Verre-Müller. She summoned him to lunch at Café de Flore in the Boulevard Saint-Germain. It was both useless and impossible to resist her, nobody could and he was no exception.

Yvette had been a famous French model for Chanel in the sixties and was still the most beautiful and elegant woman, tall and regal, the epitome of Parisian chic. As usual she was immaculately dressed in a black suit, Chanel of course.

As she entered the restaurant, Yvette was lavished by the waiting maître d' with the attention he reserved for his best celebrity clients. All heads turned in the fashionable restaurant as after settling her at her usual table, Yvette immediately stood and waved to her handsome, famous son who was right on time.

"My darling, I'm here," she gestured, raising a bejewelled hand.

"*Bonjour maman*," said Xavier, kissing her on both cheeks and settling down to wait for her to reveal why she had called this meeting.

Xavier hoped she wasn't getting divorced again. Her third husband, a billionaire German industrialist named Heinrich Müller, was rarely seen in her company. These days he hardly saw his mother himself, as he was busy filming all over France.

After a few minutes of catching up, with only limited patience for small-talk when she had something on her mind, Yvette revealed her true intentions for the luncheon.

"Darling, I hear you've bought a hovel in some godforsaken place in the countryside. I was wondering if there was a reason why you are keeping this secret from me?" Yvette was direct as always.

"What are you talking about?" Xavier had not seen his mother during the months waiting for the sale to be finalised.

"You know darling, a woman maybe? You are thirty-five now and it's time for my first grandchild."

"No, no woman." At least not yet, not that he was certain of.

"So why the house, Xavier, if it's not a woman?" Yvette wasn't so easily convinced.

"I know you'd like to see me married off, but really, I'm quite happy as I am. The house is very special and a bargain, so I couldn't miss the opportunity." Xavier had no buyer's remorse whatsoever; the property was stunning and even Yvette would think so.

"Ok, I'll accept that," Yvette conceded, before playing her ace card. "If there really is no woman, then I want you to join me for a little dinner party this evening at the Champ de Mars apartment."

"No more matchmaking. I'm not interested,"

Xavier stated firmly.

"Darling, I'm so proud of you. You can't blame me for wanting to show you off to my friends. The Countess de Savory will be there with her very attractive, single and rich daughter. You remember Victoria? I've assured them you're coming since you're in town. Just indulge me this one time, please for me," she cajoled.

"My case is packed and I'm leaving as soon as we've finished here." He held his ground, knowing she would go on until she got her way.

"One more night won't hurt you, Xavier! You can be so spoilt and selfish sometimes. You never visit, you hardly call or write. You are my only child and I am constantly lonely, as if you care!" Yvette could be very dramatic when it suited her.

Xavier sighed deeply, thinking about the lengths she would go to in order to get what she wanted. Yet it was true, one extra night to please her wouldn't make a huge difference to his burgeoning relationship with Alex, but it would appease his mother and that was its own reward.

If only he had taken Alex's telephone number, but it couldn't be helped. He would have felt better if he could contact her and explain his absence. He was sure she was thinking of him, as he was of her and he couldn't wait to get back and pick up where they had left off. He was almost certain this was the start of something special, at least he hoped so.

***

By Wednesday, Elaine was still unaccounted for and had been missing for three days and Sophie was frantic. She couldn't remember any time that her sister hadn't spoken to her for this long, nor had she been in to work. She could have called home if she was in Paris with Xavier. There was definitely something wrong; as the time dragged on she was more convinced than ever that something terrible had happened to Elaine.

Charles had called her after his visit to the de Verre house on Tuesday and told her that the place was closed with no sign of life. It seemed most likely that the selfish Elaine had simply taken off with the de Verre playboy, without any consideration for her family's distress. Sophie did not believe that and told him so.

"Charles, something is not right. I can feel it, you must believe me. Please take it seriously!" she begged. "Elaine would have been able to call me by now, at least once. I've tried her mobile and it goes straight to voicemail. She never switches the damn thing off; she's always texting or calling someone and none of her friends have heard from her."

"Calm down Sophie. How do you know that?"

"Because I have checked Charles!" she screamed.

“I have tried everyone she knows that I could get hold of. What do you think I have been doing for the last three days?”

“Ok, ok,” he soothed, although he was quite surprised by the strength of her outburst.

“Can’t you find a number in Paris for Xavier de Verre or his television company? At least check him out, surely the chief of the gendarmerie can do that!” Sophie was exasperated, but she seemed to be getting through at last.

Charles had to admit that Sophie was not normally the kind of person to create a drama, but he wasn’t sure how far he could seriously take this. He had made some enquiries into Xavier de Verre but they hadn’t revealed anything of interest, apart from the usual Google nonsense about his famous family and his television show. He had no criminal record or any shady dealings, which was more than could be said for that politician father of his.

It was hard to find the black-listed number of a celebrity unless there was an official investigation underway. If he wanted to file Elaine as a missing person, he would have to involve the police in Laval. Right now, he was unwilling to take that step; mostly for fear of making himself look a fool when she breezed back in a day or two. No, he’d give it another twenty-four hours and then report it himself.

Sophie was not pleased but she didn't want to undermine the authority of his position in the community, so she was forced to accept his decision.

Chapter 13

Alex lounged in the sun with her book and tried to concentrate. Her thoughts kept straying back to her night of passion. She couldn't help but smile, but she wasn't so sure about Jack. His face had dropped when he walked in with that armful of flowers and saw her standing cool and composed in the kitchen. She was sure that he had expected her to be all over him and was not impressed by her casual attitude.

Local women probably threw themselves at him, but Alex didn't care. It wasn't like she really had any feelings for him, apart from his obvious attractive looks she would not normally be interested. He certainly seemed to be keen but he was not really her type. She had to admit that she felt much more relaxed and it had certainly put her little episode with Xavier into proportion.

Alex had intended to change her ferry ticket today but that didn't seem quite so important anymore. She'd just chill and enjoy the sunshine whilst it lasted, after all, this is what she'd come here for. Despite any misgivings, her night of unbridled lust seemed to have done her some good. At least she had not thought about John in days, perhaps France had helped cure her heartbreak after all.

***

Jack however wasn't so happy. He had thought Alex was different, been taken in by her good-girl act. He'd had his fill of selfish bitches who used him. Why did this always happen to him? She'd be sorry when she finally came back for more and she would, they all did. He smiled to himself at the thought of how different it would be next time. She'd had her chance and ruined it.

Jack continued to drink from the bottle of whiskey stashed under the reception desk, taking steady swigs throughout the day. He wanted to get Alex out of his head but he could not stop thinking about her. Images of her naked body as he pounded her kept invading his mind. By the evening he was desperate for distraction, trying hard to keep the erection that had been with him on and off all day under control. He decided he would pay Jayne a visit, at least she'd be grateful.

It was late and Jayne was in her dressing gown. She was thinking about going to bed, when she heard a car pull up in the drive of her remote cottage. She wasn't used to visitors and especially not at this time of night. Her heart leapt when she saw Jack swaggering across her drive. She wished she had been wearing something slightly more attractive, but she couldn't think of anything in her practical wardrobe that would have done.

"Jack," she said, opening the door. "What are you doing here? It's very late, I was just about to go to bed."

"Well, I like the idea, you bad girl," Jack smiled, taking it as an invitation as he clutched at her, made a grab and kissed both her cheeks, swaying slightly.

"I come bearing gifts," he went on, as he released her, strode past and pulled a bottle of wine out of the bag and placed it on her scruffy kitchen table.

"Come on girl, get the corkscrew," he demanded, eyeing her figure as she scuttered past. "You look great by the way. I like women in dressing gowns, especially when they have nothing on underneath."

Jayne felt her cheeks colour as she gave him the corkscrew and two glasses, then gestured towards the front room.

"Shall we go in there?" she suggested. "It's a bit better, more finished. There's still a lot of work to do but we ran out of money. I'm sorry about the state of the place."

"There you go again," he said, following her through to the tiny sitting room dominated by a huge, plasma screen television.

"Always saying sorry when you haven't done anything wrong. Yet," Jack smirked.

Jayne sat nervously on the edge of the sofa whilst Jack made himself at home, rifling through Tom's CD's until he found an old Motown compilation and put it on the elaborate stereo system.

"Old Tom certainly likes his toys, I can see where the money went. On the really important things," he added nastily.

Jayne felt increasingly more uncomfortable but at least the wine was helping. Jack had knocked back his glass quickly and poured himself another. She could see that he was quite drunk already and thought he must have been at it all day.

The whiskey this morning had made her feel quite sick and woozy, but clearly he had pushed straight through and was heading towards oblivion. She wondered what had happened to set him off on an all-day drinking session.

Jayne was not pleased by Jack's sudden appearance. She could admit to herself that she fancied him rotten, but it was a bit cheeky to just turn up on her like this. Although she would hardly have found the courage to invite him herself, plus she was a married woman. She had stayed faithful to Tom throughout the marriage and until recently believed he had done the same. How had her life turned out like this?

She was not a woman scorned, but she was abandoned by her husband and she had been lonely for a long time. Now she had this big hunk who had invited himself round and was drinking in her living room. She wanted him physically, but she found him brash and abrasive and he made her feel uneasy, slightly on edge and even threatened. This factor only added to the sexual excitement and Jayne felt thoroughly confused.

Jack threw back another glass of wine and started dancing provocatively around.

"Come on, Jayne," he said, reaching out for her to join him. "Lighten up and enjoy yourself."

"I don't think so, Jack."

Sensing opportunity, Jack grabbed her hand.

"Come dance with me. You know you want to. You know you want me," he said, roughly pulling her towards him.

"Jack please, you're drunk! I think you should go before this goes any further." Jayne tried to draw away.

"I don't think so," he said, pulling her closer and searching for her mouth.

He drew her hungrily against him for a hot embrace, clutching at her. She could smell and taste the alcohol as he kissed her, thrusting his tongue deep inside her mouth. She made a half-hearted effort to pull away, but her knees were buckling and her resistance crumbled. He pulled open the old dressing gown which dropped to the floor.

"Very sexy," he said playfully, looking down at her faded cotton nightdress.

"Arms up," he ordered, as if she were a child he was undressing.

In one quick move he pulled the nightdress up and over her head, until she was standing naked before him. Her body was good for her age and he was pleased with himself for recognising this little treat when he found it.

"Much better," he commented.

He pulled her towards him and began kissing her deeply, groping at her breasts. It was no use, she was like putty in his experienced hands. Nobody had touched her in two years and before that, Tom's clumsy efforts had left her cold and unfulfilled. Jack was right, she did want this. She willingly let him turn her round, facing away from him, kneeling on the sofa.

Jack undid his trousers, got out his swollen cock and pushed it straight into her from behind. She was taken by surprise by such a sudden and unexpected entry. She clung to the back of the sofa crying out, as he pushed himself into her again and again. He smacked her thrusting buttocks.

"Dirty slut!" he shouted, as he pumped and smacked in rhythm.

Suddenly he turned her round, pulled back her head and standing in front of her, pushed his ejaculating penis into her mouth. Just like that it stopped.

"I've got to go, Jayne," he said, putting himself away and doing up his flies.

"Can't leave the guests unattended all night," he added by way of an explanation, as he immediately departed.

He left Jayne sitting there naked and stunned; sticky, bitter cum in her mouth, on her face and in her hair. She became aware of the song lyrics in the background.

'*Now that you're gone, all that's left is a band of gold,*' was playing on Tom's stereo.

All that her humiliated mind could think was that he didn't even trouble himself to get undressed. Perhaps this was what the kids meant by 'fuck and run'. Well now she knew too, she started to sob.

***

Xavier had known the young Lady Victoria de Savory since childhood as a family acquaintance, because her parents owned the villa next door to theirs in Saint-Jean-Cap-Ferrat. He was pleasantly surprised to find her all grown up.

She was striking, tall and willowy, with exquisite bone structure and a full pale mouth. He found it hard not to notice her long, silky chestnut hair, falling softly over her naked shoulders. Her vivid green eyes were complemented by the colour of her silk designer dress and the large real emeralds that circled her creamy neck and sparkled on her wrist.

They sat next to each other at the large antique table chatting amicably, occasionally joining in with the general conversation amongst the other ten distinguished guests.

His mother looked pleased and played the perfect hostess, as each carefully chosen course followed the other. The wines and food complementing each other with the precision achieved by years of entertaining experience. All her dinners were planned by her professional chef and sommelier and served by her loyal but long-suffering staff.

As the evening drew to a close, Xavier extended a friendly invitation to Victoria to visit him in Lassay. They had got on well, plus she loved riding. She had heard of the area, famous for the quality of the horses raised and the location of the Haras national du Pin stud farm.

He returned to his studio feeling relaxed. He was

amazed that in one week he had met two equally beautiful and intelligent women, it must be a record. It had been nice to be able to talk in his native language to Victoria, who though English, spoke flawless Parisian French. She had looked stunning at dinner he reflected, different from the girl he remembered. Her elegant beauty, self-confidence and sharp wit was in such contrast to the gentle laughter and sensuous looks of Alex.

Chapter 14

Xavier arrived back in Lassay on Thursday morning, throwing open the windows and letting the sunlight flood into his home. He had made excellent time, really pushing the Porsche as he raced back to his country retreat. Later he would drop in on Alex and apologise for his hasty departure.

Xavier decided to walk into the village and buy a few provisions he needed. He was approaching the town square, when a woman he didn't know rushed up to him. She quickly introduced herself as Sophie, Elaine Dubois's sister.

"Monsieur de Verre, what's happened to Elaine? I know she was with you last Sunday night. Please tell me she's been with you since then!" She was half-hysterical and on the verge of tears.

"I'm sorry, madame, I don't know what you're talking about." Xavier was deeply concerned by Sophie's very evident distress. "I haven't seen Elaine since I left her at the nightclub."

"Oh my God!" she cried out.

Sophie collapsed onto the little stone wall outside the town hall and began sobbing in earnest.

"I knew something was wrong. I told Charles, but he wouldn't listen to me. Now it's too late, too late!" she wailed.

Xavier tried to place a comforting hand on her shoulder, but she pushed it away.

"Leave me alone! Don't touch me, you monster!" she shouted angrily at him.

A few of the locals stopped and regarded the scene. A couple of older ladies recognised Sophie and went over to her, pushing past Xavier to offer their assistance and soothe her.

"She's gone," she continued to cry out in despair. "Elaine is missing. Please somebody help me. Call my brother, call Charles," she begged through fast-falling tears, her face a picture of anguish.

***

Charles was at his desk in the Lassay gendarmerie headquarters when he received a garbled message that he had to come now; his sister was in town, broken down and crying.

When he arrived a few minutes later, he could not glimpse Sophie yet, but saw Xavier de Verre standing helplessly by amongst the crowd of villagers gawping. He made his way through and went straight to his sister.

"Sophie," he said gently, whilst glaring at de Verre. He knew this man would cause nothing but trouble, his type always did.

"Sophie, come with me. I'll call Jacques, come along," he said, throwing de Verre another menacing look.

"Don't go anywhere," Charles pointed a finger at him. "I'll be coming to see you soon monsieur, believe me," he said, steering the sobbing Sophie towards his car, away from prying eyes.

Xavier was shocked, what on earth was happening here? He felt the stares of hostility and accusation. He was suddenly aware they all seemed to think he was involved in the disappearance of a young woman. The suspicion and menace on their faces reminded him he was an outsider here, not known and not trusted. He retreated self-consciously from the growing crowd, his shopping long-forgotten.

On his walk back to the house, he went over in his mind the last time he'd seen Elaine. She had been drunk and all over him, before dancing with Jack and he took his chance and escaped. Jack might know something; he was the only person he could think to ask, but the last thing he wanted to do was walk back into town and find him. The hotel had to be in the phone book or online, he would go straight home as quickly as possible and find the number.

Jack had been watching this drama unfold from the open door of the hotel. He saw the gendarme arrive and take away the collapsed woman. Even after their departure, the townsfolk were still gossiping, heads together chuntering. This was a massive event for the village. A girl they had known all their lives had disappeared, the niece of the chief of the gendarmerie no less.

Jack had clocked Xavier de Verre in the crowd, then watched his tall frame sloping off in the direction of his house. He was getting away from the little groups of men and women who had formed and were sending hate in his direction. He noticed that they turned their heads to follow his progress as he departed, fascinated with him even as they suspected and blamed him.

Jack casually approached from the other side of the town square.

"What's going on?" he enquired to a group of men.

"It's that Elaine Dubois, she's missing," one responded. "She was always a bad one that girl, caused her father and brother no end of trouble!"

"That was her sister, poor woman, crying and wailing," another commented. "I heard her say that Elaine had been with Xavier de Verre the night she disappeared."

"Probably been throwing herself at him because he's famous, the silly tart," the first old man continued, not impressed.

Jack said nothing. Over their heads he saw Alex's car pull up and park in the square. She got out looking stunning in a little pink dress and he felt a familiar stirring, before his face clouded over. He deliberately headed towards her then refused to acknowledge her, passing by as if she were invisible.

"Hi," she tried to greet him. Alex was surprised, then angry when Jack went sailing past and ignored her.

"Jack wait!" she called, as she followed after him.

He stopped without turning round and she walked up to his broad back.

"Jack, what's wrong with you?" she asked perplexed. "Have I done something to upset you?"

"Nothing's wrong," he said flatly, turning and giving her a cold stare.

"I don't understand why you just walked straight past me. Would you like to explain yourself?" Alex asked, trying to keep her voice level but feeling increasingly irritated by his attitude.

"It's you who needs to explain your behaviour," he said sharply.

"What are you talking about Jack? If it's about the other night, I'm sorry. It was a mistake that should never have happened. I was drunk and upset, what else can I say? I apologise, ok?"

"No, Alex, I don't think that it is 'ok', as you put it!" Jack was furious. "I've seen you."

"Seen me doing what?" she was perplexed.

"I have CCTV in the bedrooms of the hotel. Don't deny what you've been up to, because I've seen the video with my own eyes!" he finished triumphantly.

"Alright, I'm completely lost now," and she was. "I don't understand anything you're talking about. I've never set foot in your hotel!"

"If you say so Alex, but really there's no point in lying. I have the evidence on camera," he smiled at her in a decidedly sinister way. Clearly, he was the one who had lost it.

Suddenly he shouted at her. "Besides I don't care! You mean nothing to me. You are not my mother."

"That's it!" Alex shouted back. "I don't have to put up with this shit. You're nuts! Don't bother speaking to me again!"

She stormed back to her vehicle in a rage, slamming the car door shut, breathing deeply as she opened the windows. She was red-faced and bursting with adrenaline from the confrontation, trying to gain control, but seriously angry. What on earth was all that about?

She tried to work through the bizarre exchange that had just taken place. Jack was obviously more upset than she had realised. He was clearly pissed at her for being unreceptive to the flowers and breakfast, there could be no other explanation. Maybe she had been a bit cruel, but she didn't want him to mistake what had happened between them as something more than it was.

This kind of behaviour though was completely new to Alex. What the hell was he talking about? He seemed to have totally lost his grip on reality. How had she not noticed how seriously creepy and unhinged he was? She couldn't believe she had slept with him, and worse, loved every shameful minute.

As Alex drove out of the village, she spotted Xavier's car in his drive. So he was back now, but was Elaine with him or not? She instantly decided to stop, she might as well get it all over and done with on one day. Then she would stay away from these people, mind her own business and book her ferry ticket back home. Enough was enough.

Xavier had been pacing his kitchen, very agitated and upset. The response of the villagers had given him an inkling of what was to come in terms of the immediate future. Elaine was missing and he'd been one of the last people to see her. He very much needed her to turn up alive and well and not be associated with any scandal, for the sake of his family as well as his own career.

Xavier was genuinely concerned for the girl. A lot had happened since Sunday night. She had been missing that whole time and nobody had noticed or tried to get in contact? There was more going on here than he understood, but he was very distressed at being dragged into it from one bad decision. He was also uncertain how it would progress from here, but he knew that he should expect a visit from the gendarmerie as threatened.

Xavier could account for his trip to Paris, but not his walk home from the club. He racked his brains to think if he'd seen anyone on that long walk that might be able to verify where he'd been and at what time, but the country roads had been deserted at that hour of the morning. He could not think of a single person who might have spotted him.

Xavier heard the knock at the door and straightened up, expecting to see gendarmes. He was relieved as he opened the door to find Alex standing there instead. She was radiant in her pink sundress, her hair pinned up loosely on top of her head, a smart pair of Dolce & Gabbana sunglasses shading her hazel eyes.

"Thank God, it's you Alex!" said Xavier, looking in

both directions over her shoulder, as he pulled her into the hallway.

"I can't believe what's happened. Have you spoken to Jack?" Xavier asked immediately and Alex cringed.

"Sorry to just turn up, Xavier." She ignored his question, determined to get this resolved once and for all. "Is Elaine here?"

"No, I don't know anything about Elaine, except she has disappeared," Xavier replied. She could tell instantly he was telling the truth.

"Wait, so she's definitely missing? She was not with you?" Alex was stunned by the enormity of her mistake.

"Why does everyone think she was with me? I was in Paris," he insisted.

"Without Elaine?" Alex needed to be sure.

"Of course. Why would I take Elaine to Paris with me?" Xavier was genuinely surprised by their assumptions in town. Now Alex had also thought the same?

"Xavier, are you telling me that nobody has seen Elaine since Sunday night?" Alex suddenly forgot about her own personal angst.

"Yes, that's exactly what I am telling you," Xavier was frustrated. "I've only just found out, now I'm waiting to be questioned by the gendarmerie. Has Jack said anything to you?"

Xavier waited expectantly, but it took a moment to process this in her muddled brain. What could she say? She felt terrible that Xavier had been falsely accused and she herself was guilty of this. She had believed Jack so easily when he planted the idea that Elaine was with Xavier. Was it him who had manipulated her or had she been blinded by jealousy?

No, she realised, suddenly remembering that it was the gendarme the day before outside Xavier's house. She had just assumed because they were both gone and Jack had let her think that. How could she have been so stupid?

"Nobody knew Elaine was missing. Sorry Xavier, but Jack kind of intimated that she'd gone with you to Paris," Alex confessed apologetically. She had to tell him the truth, to warn him.

"God, it's getting worse by the minute! You didn't really believe that I would just run off with Elaine, Alex, did you?" The look on her face confirmed that that was exactly what she had thought.

"Come on, let's calm down. I'll get you a coffee or better still some tea," she soothed, as they went into the kitchen.

"How did you find out Elaine was missing?" Alex asked.

"I went to Lassay and bumped into her sister. She stopped me and broke down when she found out the girl was not with me. It's awful but I've no idea what happened to her. I was out with them that night, but only because they told me you were meeting us," Xavier continued. "I left the club alone when I realised you definitely weren't coming. I can't imagine what has happened to her."

"Was she drunk when you left? Was she with any other men?"

"She was very drunk, she kept rubbing herself against me. I was getting annoyed with her; I don't like that kind of thing. Now nobody has seen her since that night. I walked home alone Alex. There were no other people that I can remember, so it looks very bad for me and I'm sure it won't end here."

Xavier held his head in his hands with frustration, the waiting was fraying his nerves.

"I was hoping that Jack could remember if he saw her leave with anyone. Maybe you should go Alex, I don't want you mixed up in this."

"I wouldn't dream of leaving you to face this alone. Call Jack at the hotel and see what he remembers," she suggested.

"There was no answer before, I'll try again." Xavier

reached for the phone.

At the hotel, Jack could hear the phone ringing. He guessed it would be Xavier or worse still, Alex. He had no intention of picking up. Let them sweat, he thought, they deserved it.

Chapter 15

Captain Dubois called a meeting at the gendarmerie headquarters in Lassay. When his officers were assembled, he announced that his sister was missing and he needed a search party organised. He assigned his deputy chief, Captain Gaston, to co-ordinate their efforts and get started immediately.

It had been a terrible scene with Sophie, now waiting safely in his office. She had cried and beaten at his chest, blaming him for everything. He was relieved when Jacques turned up and took his weeping wife home.

"There's nothing you can do here, Sophie," Charles insisted. "I need to get on with things now. I have work to do."

She'd refused to go at first, but Jacques had managed to persuade her that it was the most sensible thing to do. Charles still had the awful task of phoning his parents ahead of him. Instead, he looked in his business card holder for a particular number and dialled.

***

Inspector Giles Bonet was sitting with his feet up on his desk at the police headquarters in Rennes, looking out of his office window. He was a large man; the remnants of youthful good looks walked with him, although this was no longer a frame that went running. He still felt strong, but was clearly past his prime and pushing retirement.

He was hoping that the fine weather would hold out for his annual holiday. His wife Monique was pestering him to go to the island of Réunion. He was sure that his daughters had put her up to it. What was wrong with Saint-Malo?

They had been going there for the past thirty-five years. He liked the little static home by the beach they rented; he could relax, he knew people and most of all he hated flying. He'd done enough of that during his time in the army. If he never saw another foreign place again, he wouldn't care. Saint-Malo suited him just fine.

Had Monique forgotten the cost of their youngest daughter's wedding? It would take years to recover financially, but at least both girls were now married off to good men with secure jobs. What more could a father ask for? The ringing phone cut in on his thoughts.

"Bonet," he answered.

"It's Captain Charles Dubois. I am chief of gendarmerie, Lassay-les-Châteaux."

"Yes captain, what can I do for you?" Giles replied.

"I know this is not the usual chain of command Inspector Bonet, but I met you once at a regional law enforcement conference and I retained your card. I have a very delicate situation here in Lassay," Charles started, and Bonet was intrigued.

"A woman has been missing without trace since Sunday night. Her name is Elaine Dubois. She also happens to be my youngest sister," said Charles, choking on the words. He had to take a moment to clear the lump that had formed in his throat.

"As a missing person case, I should report it to Laval police because I have too personal an interest," Charles explained unnecessarily.

"So why are you calling me?" Bonet asked.

"There is a particular reason. I have a potential suspect who may be involved with her disappearance, who I have not yet questioned," Charles paused. "To make matters worse, it happens to be the television naturalist Xavier de Verre." He gave Bonet a moment to digest the implications of this.

"Leave it to me, Captain Dubois," he replied, immediately recognising the famous name from his past. "I will clear things here and be with you as soon as possible. Have you organised your men into search parties?"

"Yes inspector," Charles was relieved.

Bonet would take charge from here. He knew he had done the right thing by calling him, as he remembered he had once worked as part of the security team for Jean de Verre. He had an excellent reputation and would know exactly how to handle the investigation.

"We know the general area that needs to be covered and it should stay light for some hours. Many of my men are local so they're familiar with the terrain. I have allocated my deputy chief responsibility for co-ordinating the search. I'll wait here to update you when you arrive."

Giles put down the phone and played with his moustache, pulling the ends into perfect points. He would have to tread very carefully and hoped that Dubois was wrong about his suspicions. He had seen Xavier de Verre on television, it was one of his favourite programmes. The young man looked fit and healthy and came across as very likeable.

When he came out of the army, he had joined the service de la protection (SDLP), a special unit of the police responsible for the safety of French VIP's and foreign dignitaries, both at home and abroad. He had been assigned to the up-and-coming politician Jean de Verre, and also knew his wife Yvette, having guarded the couple on formal occasions before their divorce. He had met Xavier a few times as a youth.

Bonet wondered whether Captain Dubois was calling him because he mentioned that he had worked with Jean de Verre at whatever conference he was referring to. He could get in contact with the de Verre family whenever he needed to.

After he stopped working as a VIP bodyguard for the protection service, Bonet spent ten years in Paris with the central judicial police investigating serious crimes, including murder cases. This was the main reason he would be able to pull rank, even though he was quietly serving out his last few years until retirement in the provinces. He had more experience than almost anyone within three hundred kilometres.

Firstly, he would have to get the investigation officially assigned to him. He called to get the necessary clearance for his intervention. His commander agreed he would be the perfect choice because of his past connection to the family and experience of handling publicity and attention from the press.

Before leaving for Lassay, he called his wife Monique to advise her to put dinner on hold and not wait up for his return.

"Can't someone else go Giles?" she moaned, "I might as well not bother cooking for you at all! When will all of this stop?"

"Not before I retire. Monique, you know what it's like, it's my job," he gave the usual answer. This was a long-standing issue within their marriage and no good would come from prolonging the conversation.

"See you in the morning," he finished firmly, then hung up.

Giles left the office and got into his unmarked car. He listened to classical music and chain-smoked Gauloises cigarettes on the journey. The smoking helped him concentrate even though he had supposedly given up two years ago.

He could only imagine Yvette de Verre's reaction if her son was involved with a dead girl. He felt certain in the pit of his stomach, that sense of dread. This was not just a missing person; this was a murder case, he could smell it.

Chapter 16

News of Elaine's disappearance spread like wildfire throughout the close-knit community. Families speculated as to the fate of the wayward Elaine Dubois, not surprised she had come to a bad end. They refused to let their daughters out alone in case a predator was on the loose.

The local men jammed the phone lines to the gendarmerie offering their services and were directed to the meeting place for search parties. They would be allocated their areas and guided by the local chasse, professional hunters with trained dogs.

Charles Dubois waited patiently for the arrival of Giles Bonet. Giles had called to let him know he was on the way, and warned him to wait to question Xavier de Verre until he arrived. He reminded him that his father was a politician with powerful friends and connections.

Xavier himself was still pacing his home, waiting for the gendarmerie to come and question him. He had tried to phone Jack a number of times and had eventually given up, he would get no answers from him.

Just after 6.00pm, the knock that he was dreading finally came. Xavier opened the door to face two very different men; the gendarme from this afternoon, accompanied by a large, dark-haired man in a slightly rumpled suit.

"Good evening, Monsieur de Verre." Bonet took the lead. "This is Captain Charles Dubois. I am Inspector Giles Bonet from Rennes police."

"Xavier de Verre," he replied automatically. There was something familiar about Bonet that he couldn't quite place.

"Please come in," he invited them into the drawing room and offered them a seat.

Giles took in the exquisite furnishings of the restored room. Very nice, he thought to himself, even to his eye it was impressive. He smiled reassuringly at the nervous young man sitting before him.

"Can I get you anything? Coffee or water?" Xavier asked, but they both declined.

"We are here to ask you some questions concerning the disappearance of Elaine Dubois," Bonet opened with. "I must tell you that if you would prefer to have this conversation at the gendarmerie in the presence of your solicitor, then we can agree on a time and make an appointment."

"No, I'm happy to answer your questions. I've done nothing wrong inspector." Xavier wanted this nightmare over and done with.

"Very well, then let us begin with your account of Sunday night. As accurately as possible please, giving times if you can remember. Anything could be important," Bonet instructed him.

Xavier went through his recall of the night with as much detail as possible. When he came to the part about leaving the club and walking home, Bonet raised his eyebrows.

"You walked all that way at night? More than ten kilometres?" Bonet repeated and Xavier nodded. "Do you have any idea what time you arrived here?"

"That is the problem, I can't remember exactly," Xavier admitted. "It was just starting to get light so I would estimate around 4.00am to 5.00am."

"So that would mean you walked from La Pellu to this house in approximately three or four hours? That is quite a distance Monsieur de Verre, for somebody who is unfamiliar with the area."

"I'm used to walking inspector, it's part of my job."

"Yes, I'm familiar with your television programme." Bonet accepted his answer, for now. "So to confirm, you left Elaine Dubois dancing with Jack Winter and that was the last time you saw her?"

"Yes inspector."

Xavier found it impossible to judge whether they believed him or not. Charles Dubois had not spoken a word. He seemed to be almost in shock, stunned into silence. He was startled by his mobile phone ringing, and stood up and went to the window facing away from the room.

"Very well, we're on our way," he turned, his face the colour of ashes. "Inspector Bonet, we need to leave immediately."

Giles looked into Charles' eyes, he could see the man was obviously shaken and knew the moment he had been dreading had arrived. With that, both men excused themselves and made for the door.

"Monsieur de Verre, it may well be necessary to speak with you again and record a formal statement."

"Of course, Inspector Bonet. I'll be here."

Xavier noticed Bonet place a consoling hand on Dubois' shoulder. My God, what now? Certainly it seemed like terrible news, based on the look on his face after he received the call. Suddenly it clicked, Charles Dubois, Elaine Dubois. The gendarme was her brother.

***

Alex had waited in the kitchen during the visit from the gendarmerie, and she could barely believe or even comprehend what was happening. Yesterday she had been happy and much more in control of her emotions. She'd decided to forget Xavier and Jack, finish her holiday and get back to her real life in London.

Today everything had changed again, part of her just wanted to run away from it all. Xavier hadn't been with Elaine? That was a shocking revelation. How much of her behaviour had been induced by jealousy over something which did not even exist? So then where was Elaine? What had happened to her? And what about Jack? What had he seen or heard? In fact, where was Jack?

They had called the hotel several times and each time were forwarded to the machine. It had to be serious, Elaine had been missing since Sunday night. That was four days in this blistering heat, even if she'd just passed out on her way home, she could have come to some harm. She could have got lost, had an accident or a fall after leaving the nightclub drunk. So many questions, Alex couldn't just walk out and leave Xavier to this ordeal.

When Xavier returned to the kitchen, he was pale underneath his bronzed skin. His tight mouth and furrowed brow told her that the meeting with the police had not gone well. He explained to Alex they had received a call and left suddenly.

"For God's sake, Xavier! This is really serious, what are you going to do?" Alex couldn't help saying.

"I don't know Alex," he was devastated. "I tried to tell the police, but I just can't recall exactly what happened. I was drunk too!"

"What do you remember then?" Alex asked. "Go through it in your mind."

"After I left and started walking, I felt ill and sat down for a while. Presumably on the side of the road, but which road, I don't know. I just remember thinking to keep my bearings and head south-west, that it would lead me to Lassay eventually."

"Go on," she urged.

"Honestly, none of it would have been familiar to me, I don't know the area well enough. What really bothers me is that I can barely remember walking home at all, or getting to bed. I was woken the next day by the phone ringing. It was my agent."

"Do you think you should call your solicitor for advice at least?" Alex suggested.

She was worried that events would quickly get out of hand once the press got wind of the story. This was a small village, things like this just didn't happen in Lassay. It was about to be exposed with potentially epic consequences; a famous television celebrity, a missing local girl. Xavier needed to prepare himself rapidly because a storm was coming that could damage them all.

"Do you think I did anything Alex? Could I have hurt her?" Xavier looked very directly into her eyes.

"Don't be crazy Xav, I could never suspect you. Besides we are talking about her as if she is dead and we don't even know what has happened yet. There could be another explanation," Alex attempted to reassure him. "Try to stay calm, but really I think you need some legal advice. Call your people and get help."

"You're right Alex, what would I do without you?"

He crossed to the other side of the kitchen where she was standing, then pulled her towards him, burying his face in her sweet-smelling hair and breathing in the fresh fragrance. Alex wrapped her arms around his back and held him very tightly.

"I'm so sorry, Xav," she whispered, shame and embarrassment about what had happened with Jack flooding through her mind in a hot rush of guilt. How could she have slept with him? How could she have been so stupid and so wrong?

Xavier gently lifted her face to his and their lips met. Alex looked into those deep blue eyes, so filled with apprehension but also desire, and melted into him. All her resistance and stress just evaporated, as they sank to their knees as one, continuing to kiss each other.

The strength of her passion and need to blend completely into him was shocking, she'd never felt it before. She rapidly undid his shirt buttons, kissing across his strong chest. His hands gently feeling the contours of her body, her shoulders and the small of her back, pulling her even closer to him.

Alex didn't know how long they had been on their knees kissing but they just couldn't stop. All their pent-up, emotional turmoil tumbling out of them, their passion building up wildly towards their primal need as they clutched at each other.

Ringing, Alex could hear ringing somewhere far away.

"The phone!" cried Xavier, tearing himself away from her and rushing to answer.

Alex could hear French conversation coming from the hallway but couldn't focus her mind to listen so she sat and waited. Xavier returned and gave Alex his hand to help her up, he looked serious and the moment had gone.

"Alex, it was my mother," Xavier disclosed. "For whatever reason she has decided to pay me a visit and will be here tomorrow. This is all I need!"

“Does she know about any of this?” Alex was surprised at his exasperation.

“Of course not. I didn’t even know about this.”

Alex was silent, worried that she had annoyed him.

“My mother is not exactly low-profile,” Xavier went on. “I must take care of a few things before she arrives. I will call my family solicitor, Maître Honoré, and see what has to be done.”

“Of course, Xav,” Alex responded, but felt all the magic of those precious few moments disappear.

Xavier made the calls to his agent first and then his solicitor. Maître Honoré advised him to inform his father immediately, impressing upon him the urgency to consolidate the family stand. It was not only his reputation that was on the line. His schedule was very full, but he would be there as soon as possible.

Xavier dutifully phoned his father and explained the situation. He continued to pace all the way through the serious conversation that followed, accepting the inevitability of what his father was saying. Jean de Verre calmly warned him to speak to nobody without his solicitor, and Xavier neglected to mention he had already given an informal account of his evening.

His father warned him to be aware that the press would soon arrive like vultures to witness the great fall. He would organise protection for Xavier's home, as it seemed unlikely that he would be able to leave anytime soon.

Neither of them could work out why Yvette was on her way, but the timing could not be worse. Perhaps she had no idea what was going on, otherwise she would be heading towards her Caribbean retreat, not the mess she was walking into in Lassay.

"Remember, speak to nobody," his father ordered.

He met Alex in the hallway coming to fetch him as there was a knocking at the front door. They went to open it and for the second time that day, found a gendarme there.

"I've been sent by Inspector Giles Bonet, Monsieur de Verre," he announced formally. "I am to stand outside until further notice."

Xavier nodded, closed the door and returned to the kitchen with Alex.

"Perhaps it would be better if you left Alex," Xavier mentioned, with careful consideration. "I don't want you to be involved in this, especially with my mother's imminent arrival. There may well be a scene."

"Are you sure?" said Alex, feeling relieved to be able to get away and do some thinking of her own.

"I will call you as soon as I hear anything. I think maybe you should give me your telephone number this time," he smiled wryly at her.

Alex wrote it down on the kitchen notepad, stood on tip toes and gently kissed him. For a second, she felt the melting sensation from before and was sorry for the way the evening had ended. Under different circumstances who knew what might have happened, but really, what chance was there of any kind of future?

Chapter 17

As soon as he heard about the disappearance of Elaine Dubois, young Nicolas Preton responded by volunteering himself and his hunting dog for the search. He had been in the same class as her in college and worshipped her from afar, although she'd never given him a second glance.

When he arrived at the meeting place for search parties, he was allocated to an area just a few minutes from La Pellu. The teams were concentrating on the back roads and routes between the nightclub and Lassay. They would spread out as instructed a hundred meters apart, then let their dogs off the leashes and start walking in a straight line south.

Nicolas had been dropped off the back of his team leader's pick-up truck in front of a wooded copse. Only minutes later he was alerted by the frantic barking of Fitou, his massive dogue de bordeaux. Nicolas approached the animal and called him to heel. The dog had the scent and didn't want to leave his find, but reluctantly obeyed.

It was then that Nicolas saw her. He edged closer,

prickly sweat breaking out under his armpits. Suddenly he caught the same scent the dog had picked up; it was a terrible stench and made him gag. What he saw would be in his worst nightmares for many years.

He turned on his heels and ran back out of the woods onto the road, where he doubled over and was violently sick. He had been hunting since he was twelve years old, but he'd never seen anything like it. Other men quickly came running towards him.

"In there!" he pointed. "She's in there."

"Don't touch anything! Stop!" shouted the gendarme in charge of their party, but it was too late.

They rushed into the copse to find the mutilated body of the once beautiful and vibrant Elaine Dubois.

***

"Get back you idiots!" commanded Bonet, when he pulled up at the scene twenty minutes later. "You're destroying evidence!"

There were at least thirty local men who had been part of the search standing around, white-faced and shaken. He ushered them away from the body before returning to his vehicle.

"Stay in the car," he told Charles, to spare him any further suffering. He did not want the distraught man to see what he expected to find.

After his years on murder cases in Paris, he knew in this outdoor location, combined with the heat of the previous four days, the sight would be horrific. It was difficult for him to get close; he placed a handkerchief over his mouth and nose to block out the smell and without touching anything, made a general observation of the body.

She was face down in the loamy soil beneath an ancient oak. Her skimpy dress was ripped and tattered, bunched up around her waist exposing half-eaten buttocks. The flesh of both feet had been gnawed away. Her skin was discoloured and mottled, eaten away by insects and writhing with maggots. He prayed that she had died quickly.

As Bonet turned to leave, he stared straight into the stricken face of Charles Dubois who had crept up behind him.

"Come away," he said gently, but the normally cold demeanour of the chief cracked. He fell to his knees, covering his face and gave an awful primal scream.

"Why? Please God, tell me why?" echoed from the very depths of his soul.

Bonet helped him to his feet whilst motioning

to one of the waiting stunned gendarmes. It was Claude Arnaud who stepped forward to lead the chief away. The atmosphere was tense and silent and Bonet scanned the haunted faces of the search party.

These were local men with wives and daughters; they lived in a sleepy village where the most they would have experienced was a burglary or boundary dispute. This was a shocking and unthinkable crime.

Bonet took immediate control, ordering the area to be taped off. He made a call to his commander in Rennes to explain the situation; a body had been found. He requested a full forensic team to determine the cause of death as a matter of urgency.

The Rennes office was much bigger than Laval and had more resources, it didn't matter how long it took them to get here. They could use the facilities in the public mortuary in the nearby town of Mayenne.

Bonet wanted answers; he needed an experienced forensic team who knew what they were doing if he stood any chance of solving what looked like a murder at this point. What he had observed so far, convinced him that this young woman hadn't ended up here by accident.

Clearly the chief could play no further part in his

current state. His sister was the victim and he would have to deal with his grief and stay away from the investigation.

***

Captain Charles Dubois sat in the back of his official vehicle and stared out of the window at nothing in particular. He watched vaguely as Bonet ordered his men to secure the area whilst awaiting the arrival of the forensic team.

He had been a gendarme for twenty years since leaving school. He had risen to the rank of Captain, and as the local chief he had a reputation for always being professional, but aloof with his subordinates. He balanced this by being firm, upright and honest. He never joined his men for any planned social activities, preferring to retire to the solitude of his books. He lived quietly, single and alone by choice, in the house provided by the gendarmerie in the compound behind the station.

He was shocked at the enormity of his mistake. His own sister was dead, that was horrific enough. Now everyone knew he had neglected to report it for four days. He was overwhelmed by the responsibility of what he had done. Could Elaine have been saved? He would have to live with his choice and his refusal to open a missing person case. He was a broken man; his career, his family, his reputation would all be devastated.

Bonet cast a glance at the ashen face of the chief and beckoned to Officer Arnaud.

"What's your name son?" he said to the young man.

"Officer Arnaud, sir. Claude," he added.

"Arnaud, I want you to drive your chief home. Stay with him, not in his house necessarily, but close by. Keep an eye on him for me please."

"Yes sir," he nodded with understanding.

Bonet went to the chief's car window and tapped.

"Charles, roll down the window please."

Captain Dubois reacted as if in a coma, slowly obeying.

"Officer Arnaud is going to drive you home and stay with you," Bonet told him. Charles did not react.

"If there are any problems," Bonet looked straight at Arnaud, "I want you to call me immediately. Do you understand, officer?"

"Yes sir," Arnaud replied, taking the card from Bonet's outstretched hand with his contact details.

Arnaud noticed the chief was sitting in the back seat unresponsive, like a statue. Charles was mesmerised by the sky outside the window. As the car pulled away, the full expanse of the setting sun had created a spectacular show of vivid red, orange and purple. Was this the first time he'd ever noticed the beauty of a sunset?

Charles remembered the last time he had spoken to his sister. It was the day she went out with de Verre and he had lost his temper with her, put her down. He was trying to warn her, to protect her and he had failed.

Chapter 18

Jack had been steadily drinking whiskey in the Victor since the early evening. He had been waiting for the gendarmerie to get round to questioning him, it was just a matter of when. He hoped they would give Xavier a difficult time, it served him right.

The pub had been busy with groups of men filtering back since the search was called off, after the discovery of Elaine's body. Those who could not face going home alone, or who wanted to be part of the action, headed straight to the Victor. There was much speculation as to the cause of her death, although the consensus was that she had been murdered.

It was declared that none of their women were safe until the monster was caught, not one of them considering the possibility that in fact, the murderer could be sitting with them that evening. Most of these men had grown up together, it was unimaginable that any of their friends or relatives might be responsible.

Having declared that all the local men were

incapable, in their eyes, of committing any crime other than the odd bit of poaching; it was put down to the foreigners, basically anybody who hadn't been born in Lassay or the surrounding villages.

As outsiders, both Jack and Henri, the owner, caught the occasional suspicious glance from the men gathered around the tables. Jack was not intimidated by this, matching each look with a belligerent stare, defying anybody to actually approach him. Henri felt the marked atmosphere, and wished that he had hung on for that bar in Laval and not settled in a small town like Lassay.

Jack wanted to get out of there in case things turned nasty. He had expected to be interviewed at any moment, but it didn't seem likely now they had found her. The gendarmerie would probably come to the hotel tomorrow. He thought that de Verre would be their prime suspect anyway, but he intended to make certain of it.

Jack left the pub just after the party containing the stricken Nicolas Preton arrived. Nicolas wanted to go home and grieve privately, but his team had insisted that he needed a stiff drink. The tension heightened as the sight of Elaine's mutilated body was described to the other searchers already gathered there.

Henri wanted to close the bar before things got out of hand, but he didn't dare. Jack could hear the raised voices as he strolled up the street and did not envy Henri. He vaguely wondered if there would be a fight. He would have liked to break a few of those idiots' noses for the way they had been eyeing him up.

Jack felt a surge of energy at the thought, he was in the mood for some action himself. It occurred to him that there were better ways to work off the tension stored in his muscular frame, so he reached for his mobile and dialled Jayne's number but frustratingly there was no answer.

***

Back at the farmhouse, Alex carefully went over the events of the day. She wanted to go to Lassay and find Jack but it was far too late. He had some of the missing answers she was sure, but she couldn't help being concerned by the strange way he had treated her that afternoon. What did it all mean about the cameras in the hotel?

It was late and she honestly felt frightened to go anywhere. Elaine was gone, it could be dangerous outside. She locked the door and checked the house, suddenly nervous alone. She stood at the west-facing window nursing a glass of wine and looking at the final remnants of the beautiful sunset. Nature was so magnificent, impervious and oblivious to the suffering going on all around.

Alex could not settle down and there seemed

little chance of sleep. She couldn't stop thinking about poor Elaine and wanted to know what was happening. She wondered about Xavier's mother and what kind of reaction she would have when she found out about her son's predicament.

She kept remembering the feelings that overwhelmed her every time she was with Xavier. It was like some kind of illness; heart-pounding attraction but something else, she was completely drawn in. They seemed to have perfect chemistry, yet he was always just out of reach. Her emotions were pulled in two different directions, between her desire and what was left of her sanity, after the continued drama of her holiday.

She was certain Xavier had nothing to do with Elaine's disappearance, but even he admitted he could barely remember. She wondered what would have happened if she had gone along with them that night, maybe everything would have been different.

Alex was restless, but immediately on her feet when she heard a car draw up in the courtyard. She looked out of the kitchen window to see Jack heading towards her front door.

She felt her skin prickle and she realised she didn't want to be alone with him, certainly not at night, isolated like this. After this afternoon, she wasn't sure she ever wanted to see him again. Yet he might have the answers to her nagging questions. In the end, her curiosity and his loud repeated knocking sent her to open the front door cautiously.

"Jack, what on earth is going on?" were her first words.

"They've found Elaine."

"Oh my God, is she ok?" she gasped.

"No, Alex. She's dead," Jack announced grimly.

Alex felt her knees weaken and Jack took the opportunity to gain entry and led her through to the kitchen.

"Sit down. Here let me pour you another drink, you look like you need it." Jack helped her to the table.

"This is so terrible, such a young girl." Alex was devastated. "Do you know what happened to her Jack? Was it an accident?"

"Nobody knows anything yet, but someone from the search party found her earlier on. I saw him arrive at the Victor with the others, he was pretty shaken up. I left just afterwards so I don't know any details, but the locals looked a bit hostile. It's why I came here, to warn you and make sure you're ok."

"This is like some kind of bad dream," Alex replied in a daze. "I stopped by Xavier's on the way home and he's completely shocked. The police have been to ask him questions, but they left when they got a call that must have been about Elaine. Have they spoken to you yet, Jack?"

"I've been around, but nobody's come to question me. Probably tomorrow, but I don't know anything," Jack protested his innocence.

Alex hardly knew what to think anymore, so she waited for him to carry on.

"Xavier left the club first," he continued. "I think he was getting annoyed with Elaine. She was too drunk and coming on strong and he must have walked out whilst we were dancing. Elaine was all upset and tearful and wanted to go after him. I told her not to be stupid, just to leave him and try again the next day. I offered to give her a lift home, but when I turned around, she was gone."

"Let's just pray it was an accident. Otherwise, I think Xavier is in deep trouble."

"Alex, you should keep away from Xavier until we find out what happened. You don't want to get drawn into this and let's face it, we hardly know the guy. You could be in danger."

"I don't believe it was Xavier," she protested weakly.

The terrible truth of what he was saying began to sink into Alex's confused mind. Yet she had to admit that Jack could be right, none of them really knew each other, except maybe him and Elaine.

"Oh Jack, I'm so sorry. You must be terribly upset, you knew Elaine. Are you ok?" she asked, with a jolt of realisation.

"I'm ok," he said, sighing deeply and rubbing his hand over his face. "Just in shock, I guess. I know Elaine was a bit of a wild child but she was kind and lovely too. I can't believe this has happened to her, that I won't ever see her again."

"I know. It doesn't seem possible."

"God knows how her family are coping," Jack went on. "The mood in town has turned ugly; they'll be looking for a scapegoat, an outsider to blame. I think we're all in for a rough ride."

"They sent a gendarme round to Xavier's to guard him," Alex mentioned.

"Or maybe stop him from leaving town," Jack sneered, even as he reached across and gently took Alex's hand.

"Listen, I'll keep an eye out for you. If you need anything just call me at the hotel, but maybe stay out of town for the next couple of days. I suspect it will all kick off tomorrow once the press arrive. This is not the kind of thing that is going to go away quietly. Lassay is a small town, people don't get murdered here."

"Do you really think she was murdered, Jack?" Alex was alarmed.

"I don't know Alex, but it doesn't look good," Jack finished, getting up to leave. "Remember, phone if you need me, ok?"

"Thanks Jack, I appreciate that."

"It's my pleasure." Jack gave her a quick reassuring hug and went on his way.

Who could imagine after this afternoon that he could come to her rescue like that? Considering how he had behaved earlier; she was amazed at how reassured and comforted she felt by his strong presence. If Elaine had left and chased after Xavier, what exactly did happen on that walk home?

Chapter 19

Inspector Bonet waited for the forensic team at the edge of the copse. The search had long since been called off and the locals had retired home or to the bar. He had sent the gendarmes to round up the staff of the nightclub, so he could identify witnesses and begin initial questioning. He stubbed out his cigarette, noticing it was now almost completely dark. The beautiful sunset was finished and this was going to be a very long night.

He wanted to find out more about Jack Winter, but first he would talk to the staff of La Pellu to establish exactly what they had seen and heard. It was best to be armed with the correct information before rushing in and he felt the need to be cautious. He wasn't sure about Xavier de Verre, but instinctively felt that the boy had been telling the truth. Either he was the honest person he appeared to be or some sick bastard.

Bonet checked his watch and saw it was 10.15pm. It would not be too much longer before the forensic team arrived. He received a call confirming that those who had worked on Sunday night at the club had been tracked down and were waiting for him.

"Good," he replied. "Let them wait." It would make his job easier if they were suitably nervous.

A steady stream of locals had driven past to view the scene, slowing down and being moved on by the gendarmes guarding the road. The word was out, the speculation would be rife. What could he expect? He was sure if you farted in a place like this somebody would know.

His foresight told him to send a gendarme to the de Verre house as soon as they found the body, to ensure he was protected from any possible vigilante action. In an area where more than half the population were related, and as many as eighty percent owned a legitimate shotgun and various other weapons for hunting, it was best not to take any chances.

***

Charles Dubois sat in silence and complete darkness. Since he had seen his sister's dead body, unwelcome images had been invading his mind. The deformed and discoloured corpse that was etched on his brain seemed nothing to do with Elaine. How could she have ended up that way? He could hardly focus or function anymore, so complete was his grief.

He had managed to telephone and notify his

family as soon as he had been dropped back to his home. He was grateful that at least his father and Jacques had picked up their phones. He was spared from having to give the terrible news to his mother and sister, best let their men deal with it.

Both conversations had been brief, his father's shocked silence at the news his youngest child was dead, was not as hard as his brother in-law's sympathetic voice.

"I'm so sorry, Charles," Jacques told him. "Don't worry, I'll tell Sophie. Just come round when you can. Is there anything you need me to do?"

"No, but thank you, Jacques," he replied sincerely.

Officer Arnaud was outside as instructed, diligently keeping watch on the darkened house at the compound behind the gendarmerie headquarters. This was the first really serious crime to occur in Lassay during the two years he had been stationed there.

He was feeling tired, but like the other gendarmes who would be working into the early hours that night, he was anxious to do his duty. There was no movement and the curtains were closed, but he stayed at his post. He thought maybe the chief had gone to sleep; but Charles Dubois was anything but asleep, all that was registering was paralysing guilt.

***

It would be another half-hour before the forensic team arrived from Rennes, led by the distinguished and disgruntled Dr Jules Calvert. He was the very best man for the job and an excellent medical examiner, precise and meticulous with detail.

"I should have known it was you Bonet causing trouble," he said smoothly, shaking Giles' hand. "When I received the summons from God, I suspected you would be lurking around somewhere."

"Nice to see you too," said Giles, used to Dr Calvert and his changeable moods. They knew each other well and had worked together many times.

"So where is our victim?"

Bonet pointed towards the taped route to the body, barely visible through the darkness.

"Do we have any light to work with? Or are you expecting us to produce everything?" Dr Calvert demanded in his terse manner.

As the forensic team changed into their protective clothing and started to remove equipment from their van, Dr Calvert looked towards the dark copse, noting the many footprints tracking towards the body.

"Fill me in, what do we have here?" he turned to

Bonet.

"I'm not sure," he answered truthfully. "A twenty-two year old woman, sister of the chief of the local gendarmerie. She was missing for four days after a drunken night out with none other than Xavier de Verre."

"Great, so no pressure then," replied Dr Calvert. "Ok team, let's take a look." He turned to his assembled staff, gloved and ready to go, then led the way.

The forensic team got to work; they all knew exactly what needed to be done. Cables were run from the well-equipped van through the woods to the crime scene, and their large mobile lights were soon set up and illuminating the area.

Dr Calvert squatted besides the body of Elaine Dubois, whilst Bonet stood closely behind him looking over his shoulder, trying to keep out of the arcs of light flooding onto the scene. Very carefully the medical examiner made a preliminary examination, the real work would be done in the mortuary later.

Photographs were taken from every possible angle, then the team spread out to look for evidence. The exact location of each specimen was recorded, then the samples collected and placed in clear evidence bags and carefully marked. There was no trace of her mobile phone or handbag.

"What are you thinking, Jules?" enquired Bonet, when he could catch a private minute with Dr Calvert.

Normally the medical examiner would not give away any details before the official report, but aware of the potential attention this case would attract, he offered what he could.

"Four days of decomposition in excess of 25° degrees Celsius is my initial thought. What else is there to say? Both feet gone, the right hand is completely missing. Maybe we can pick something off the left hand but we'll see. Her face is structurally intact, but evidence of extensive insect and animal activity so no obvious cause of death. All to be expected under the circumstances; signs of sexual activity, torn underwear, possible violence. I'll know more later."

"Could this have been a tragic accident?" Bonet asked.

"You know I can't speculate, Giles. I have the mortuary at Mayenne notified and waiting on us. When we've finished here, we'll move her there and find you some answers. Until then if you have something better to get on with, I suggest you go do it."

***

The staff of La Pellu had been waiting ages, some

of them getting quite twitchy as the time dragged on. The place looked shabbier with the lights on and none of the usual activity to distract them. The smell of stale alcohol pervaded the air. The club receptionist, Annie, was the only person to take up her usual seat by the door. The phone rang constantly as locals called to ask her what was going on.

"Nothing. Call back later," she replied, under the watchful gaze of the gendarmes.

They were all waiting for the arrival of Inspector Giles Bonet, who finally came just before midnight. He walked straight in, immediately commanding all their attention and addressed the seated staff.

"A twenty-two year old woman, Elaine Dubois, has been found dead very close to this establishment. We have already received information to place her here between 11.00pm and 2.00am last Sunday night into Monday morning. We intend to take statements from every one of you. Please try to remember as accurately as possible anything, no matter how trivial. All the information will be valuable in assessing what happened to this young woman and will help us to eliminate you from further enquiries. Is that understood?"

They all nodded their heads, some looking more worried than others whilst a few whispered amongst themselves.

"Is there a private office that I can use?" Bonet addressed one of the gendarmes.

"Yes sir, follow me."

The office desk was cleared and chairs placed around it. Bonet produced a small tape recorder from his briefcase and placed it on top of the desk and switched it on. He clearly recorded the date, time and place and those who were present for the interviews. He chose the most senior ranking gendarme, Lieutenant Picard and asked him to assist.

"Can you write, Picard?" he asked.

"Yes sir," replied Picard.

"Fast and clearly?"

"Yes sir."

"Good. Hopefully you don't have a ruined dinner and a nagging wife waiting?" he added, reading the text message that Monique had sent him before silencing his mobile.

"No sir," responded Picard, smiling.

He liked Bonet, maybe he'd consider making the move to the big city one day. At least he appeared to have a sense of humour, which was more than could be said for the chief.

"Bring in the first one," Bonet commanded.

***

Bonet and Picard left La Pellu in the early hours. They had taken brief statements from each member of staff, but only two had known anything useful and might need to be questioned further.

"Inspector Bonet, it's very late to go home to Rennes. I have a guest room if you need it for tonight," offered Picard.

"Thank you, Lieutenant Picard."

"Please call me Michel."

"That's most kind of you," Bonet accepted. "I think we will have another long and busy day ahead of us, and I'm sure we both need the rest. We should get the medical examiner's report tomorrow, then we'll know better what we're dealing with."

"I hope the chief is alright, it's a terrible thing to witness." Picard was concerned.

"I have two daughters," Bonet added. "I can only imagine how that poor family feel."

Giles sent a text message to his wife. He knew she would not check it until the morning. She would be well and truly tucked up in bed in her curlers by now. He was grateful for Picard's generosity. He needed a few hours rest to gather his wits for the media.

He would have to prepare a statement, then get his commander's approval to proceed with the official position. He would try his best to minimise the impact on the de Verre family, assuming that the boy wasn't responsible. From what he had discovered so far, he would almost certainly be a suspect.

Tomorrow he would assemble the facts they had established and take an overall review so he could brief and co-ordinate the investigation team. He would update his commander in Rennes that based on Dr Calvert's initial thoughts, this would be a criminal investigation that would require an investigating judge and the report was to follow.

Bonet also had to deal with Charles Dubois, who weighed heavily on his conscience. He privately hoped that the chief would agree to take some time off, be with his family and stay out of the fray.

Chapter 20

Lassay awoke the next day changed by circumstances and nature. The blue skies were gone, replaced by huge storm clouds blowing in from the Atlantic. The pressure had been building, the heat now suffocating and sticky, as dry lightning flashed on the horizon.

Bonet managed only a few hours of fitful sleep, he had too much to do to rest any longer. Michel and his wife were generous hosts, laying out clean towels for his shower and providing an early breakfast to help set him up for the day.

When they arrived at the gendarmerie headquarters, the telephones were ringing constantly. Two young gendarmes looked up gratefully, not quite knowing what to do or how to proceed.

Giles took instant command, ordering them to prepare one of the larger offices to become an incident room. He requested they urgently track down a recent picture of the victim from social media, then added the two main suspects as an afterthought. He had Picard draw up a rota, allocating guard duty to the home of Xavier de Verre.

By 8.00am all were assembled at the team meeting to hear their instructions, except the chief who remained in his house, the curtains still drawn.

"My name is Inspector Bonet from Rennes police," Giles introduced himself. "I was called yesterday by Captain Dubois to investigate the disappearance and subsequent death of his sister, Elaine Dubois."

He motioned to Picard to pin a picture on the large white board behind him. The image was of a young and smiling Elaine, looking radiant and full of life.

"You are mostly local officers and some of you may have known the victim. I'm sure that you are shocked by what has happened to her." Many were nodding their heads.

"Nothing that is revealed during the course of this investigation is to be discussed outside of these walls. Absolutely nothing," he repeated with emphasis. "If I hear this order has been breached, there will be disciplinary charges. Is that understood?"

"Yes sir," several voices mumbled.

"We anticipate the press arriving imminently and we'll confirm our formal position when we schedule a conference later today. Here is another order, I expect total media silence because of the sensitive nature of this investigation."

Bonet paused to scan the faces of the officers and confirmed by their expressions that his warning had registered.

"We have already taken statements from the staff of La Pellu nightclub," Bonet went on. "The last sighting of Elaine alive was in the early hours of Monday morning. According to the club receptionist, Elaine left in a hurry just after 2.00am, obviously upset and crying. She had spent the evening in the company of two men, Jack Winter and Xavier de Verre."

"Do you mean the nature guy?" asked one of the younger gendarmes from another town.

There was a distinct murmur amongst the group as Picard wrote the famous name on the board and pinned up an image.

"Yes, that is correct. It is of the utmost importance that strict procedure must be followed," he stared them down. "Monsieur de Verre is co-operating with enquiries and is to be guarded at all times. He is extremely vulnerable to both the press and locals, who are aware that Elaine was with him the night she disappeared. It is our responsibility to protect him from harassment until we know more. I don't have to explain his background; if he is charged, then his father Jean de Verre will undoubtedly become involved."

Nobody dared say anything. Bonet had made himself clear enough, there was no room for errors or mistakes. This was a highly public case that would be closely scrutinised. When he was sure there would be no questions, he carried on as Picard put the name and picture on the board of the next suspect.

"Jack Winter is thirty-three years old, a British national who has resided in Lassay for the past year, managing his uncle's hotel Le Petit Château. According to the staff interviewed, he is a regular at La Pellu although we have not been able to establish accurately what time he left the club. We haven't interviewed him yet, but he is a distinctive and very large man, well-known locally, especially with the ladies."

The officers could understand why Elaine had gone off with either man, they both looked like handsome bastards.

"We started an interview with Monsieur de Verre that was cut short when the victim was discovered. He told us the three of them met around 9.00pm at the Victor pub here in Lassay. They stayed there drinking wine until approximately 11.00pm then went on to the nightclub La Pellu, where de Verre claimed to have left around 1.30am and walked home. The receptionist Annie verified this in her statement. According to Monsieur de Verre, he left because

Elaine made sexual advances towards him during the course of the evening, which he claims he rejected."

There was whispering and muttering in the audience, but Bonet ignored them and ploughed on.

"We need to take a statement from Monsieur Winter, who I am told speaks excellent French. I want him picked up as soon as we've finished here and brought in for questioning. Lieutenant Picard, can you take care of that?"

"Yes sir," the officer replied.

"The rest of you are to work in your usual teams of two. Arnaud, I know you're exhausted, so you go home and sleep. Officer Duval, you are to watch Captain Dubois. I'm sure you can all appreciate how difficult this is for your chief. I want him watched Duval, not further disturbed."

"Yes sir," Duval said.

"I will need statements from all the members of the Dubois family, Elaine Dubois' friends, the owner of the Victor pub, and I want to track down any customer of La Pellu who might have seen or spoken to Monsieur Winter. We need to request the victim's mobile phone records as a priority. Refer to Captain Gaston who is the senior officer on duty and he'll allocate each team a task." Bonet indicated the deputy chief, who had spruced up for the occasion in case he could get on television.

"Ok team, let's keep this professional. No matter how personally upset you feel, I expect you to do your best as gendarmes and find out exactly what happened here."

***

Yvette de Verre-Müller amazed her son by her calm resilience when she appeared early Friday morning. He had been dreading the arrival of his mother, but when he saw the chauffeured Bentley pull up, two women emerged and his heart sank. He was surprised to see the elegant form of Victoria de Savory alighting from the vehicle. Why on earth had his mother brought her?

After greeting them both and helping them in with their cases, he took them out onto the terrace to explain the seriousness of his situation.

"I did not want to tell you on the phone, *maman*. I had no idea you were bringing company," he smiled as charmingly at Victoria as he could muster.

"It's better if you both leave before the media move in. I'm sure they will be here today or tomorrow," he finished, trying to make them understand what was coming.

Amazingly both women had refused to leave, his mother insisting that at moments like this it was her duty to support her family. Yvette was more surprised when she realised he had no staff to cook and clean; in fact that seemed to be a much greater problem than the disappearance and death of a random girl. Victoria was great and took it all in her stride.

"Ok, Xav, where are our rooms?" she said, standing and moving into the hall. "If you carry up the cases, I'll get on and make sure we have linen on the beds. What about food? Do you have anything in?"

"We have enough to rustle up something for lunch," Xavier replied.

"That I can do. Don't look so surprised darling," Victoria said, noticing his expression. "I am not completely useless you know. In fact, cooking has always been one of my passions." Victoria was happy to play along and was enjoying this chance to spend time with Xavier.

Jean de Verre had called that morning to confirm the arrival of the private security team to take care of his soon-to-be besieged family. He wasn't too happy about Victoria being there, but he reasoned that if it was assumed Xavier already had a beautiful girlfriend, then it would appear less likely that he had had any connection to the dead girl. He of all people knew the importance of family unity and a public show of solidarity in the face of press intrusion.

When his father's security guards turned up at noon, they took control and stationed the gendarme outside the ornate iron gates. He had thoughtfully also sent his housekeeper Camille and a maid to look after them. She had been with the family for many years and would take over the household duties.

Xavier and his unexpected guests sat on the terrace and had lunch, eating a delicious omelette served with a huge green salad and drinking his favourite chilled chablis. At the end of their meal, Xavier took his mother's hand and kissed the back.

"Thank you *maman*, I can't tell you how much better I feel. I really appreciate you being here like this," he said, looking into her beautiful blue eyes, a mirror of his own.

"Darling, you know I love you. I wouldn't dream of leaving you here alone to deal with this. You forget I have a good deal of experience with the public and the press. After all, I was a top model and a politician's wife for many years. I have received a great deal of attention from those jackals, good and bad."

Yvette was determined to be there for her son and Xavier was grateful for her presence.

Chapter 21

Jack was up early and was very busy. The media were arriving and as the only hotel in town, Le Petit Château was rapidly filling up with bookings. He had called Jayne first thing telling her to get to work as soon as possible and offering her double pay.

After what had happened between her and Jack, Jayne hadn't returned to work for him. She had deliberately ignored his missed call from last night, but the need to earn money brought her back to reality. She was awoken by the phone ringing and through necessity, she found she could not refuse the chance to earn.

When Jayne arrived at the hotel, the reception was full of people booking in and drinking an early morning coffee, whilst discussing their pending story. Jayne figured they were mostly journalists come to find out what was happening. A missing girl was definitely newsworthy when there was a celebrity name to tag along.

There was no time for the embarrassing scene she had anticipated with Jack, it was full-on from the moment she arrived. She was in the kitchen loading used coffee cups into the dishwasher, when Jack popped his head around the door.

"Jayne, sorry love, can you watch the desk?" he asked, as if nothing untoward had happened between them. "I have to go with the gendarmes to answer some questions."

"What's going on Jack?" asked Jayne concerned.

"The girl who went missing has been found dead. That's why we have all these journalists here. I was with her the night she disappeared; not alone, but part of the group. I have to go and give them a statement."

Jayne nodded, waiting for further instructions.

"You don't have to worry about checking anybody in, we're already full," he reassured her. "Just serve drinks and write down the room numbers and I'll sort it all out when I get back. Nothing to it," and with that he turned and joined Lieutenant Picard who led him to the waiting car.

Picard drove Jack to the gendarmerie headquarters and installed him in an interview room.

"I want you in there with me for this one, Michel," said Bonet. "We have to approach this cautiously. This man, along with de Verre, is our most likely suspect."

They went into the interview room and introduced themselves to Jack. Bonet set up the tape recorder as Picard sat quietly, notepad ready. After starting the recording formally and going on the record, they began by confirming Jack's details, then came the real questions.

"Monsieur Winter, may I first say how pleased I am that you speak and understand French perfectly, it will be a great help today. What was the nature of your relationship with Elaine Dubois?" Bonet started.

"Elaine was a friend, inspector. We worked near each other, so I often saw her for a coffee or chat. Occasionally we went out in the evening to a bar or nightclub, sometimes alone but mostly with others. She was great fun and I'll miss her very much," he added carefully.

"I'm sorry to have to ask you because you must be very upset by the circumstances, but did you ever have a romantic or sexual relationship with Elaine?" Bonet pressed.

"I wouldn't say romantic, but once in a while after we'd had too much to drink, we ended up back at the hotel in bed. It wasn't serious inspector, we got on really well but it was strictly casual."

"No love affair?" Bonet enquired.

"Just friends."

"And occasional lovers?"

"Exactly," Jack confirmed. "Not for a while though."

"What happened on Sunday night?" Bonet asked. Jack hesitated for the first time, so he added for good measure. "I would like you to think very carefully, Monsieur Winter. Anything you remember might help with this investigation."

"Ok, I'll do the best I can," Jack promised. "I met Elaine and Xavier de Verre in the Victor pub about 9.00pm. We sat at the bar inside and drank a couple of bottles of red wine. Elaine looked beautiful. She'd made a real effort and was very excited because this was her first date with Xavier."

"By date, do you mean that Xavier de Verre had asked her out? To get to know her better personally?" asked Bonet.

"That is what Elaine told me."

"In that case, was it by chance that you met them?" Bonet checked.

"No, not exactly. We planned it earlier when Elaine got back from de Verre's house, that we would all meet up and go out for the night together."

"So, this was not an exclusive date? Did Monsieur de Verre know that you were coming along for the evening?"

"I'm not sure, but he didn't seem to mind," replied Jack, managing to both sound open and yet be evasive at the same time.

Bonet was immediately suspicious of his mild-mannered nature. Xavier might have been suitably anxious, but this man was almost too calm.

"How long did you stay at the Victor?"

"We left the Victor about 11.00pm and took my car to La Pellu."

"Yet you had been drinking? Didn't it worry you that you might be stopped?"

"I'm a careful drinker, inspector," Jack was smooth. I bet you are, thought Bonet, but said nothing.

"I only had one glass of wine before we left, which is why I insisted on driving." Jack didn't miss a beat. "Elaine was very impressed with his Porsche and wanted to go in his car, but I stopped him because he was clearly over the limit."

"What happened when you reached La Pellu?" continued Bonet.

"We were dancing and then we ordered a bottle of vodka. I went off to speak to some friends, as I thought they might like some time alone."

"How were Xavier and Elaine interacting during

your time at the nightclub?"

"Well Xavier seemed a bit stiff, you know like he wasn't really enjoying himself. Elaine was already quite wasted; I think she had been drinking more than both of us. She was dancing around Xavier and kept falling into him, he looked a bit put out by that and kept pushing her away. I wanted to help her with him, I knew how much it meant to her to be going out with such a famous guy. She wanted everybody to see them together."

"So, on top of what, at least two bottles of wine you then drank a bottle of vodka between you?" confirmed Bonet, his face unsurprised.

"I know, it sounds dreadful. I didn't drink more than two shots, so it wasn't that much for me at least," he added virtuously.

"Did you all continue drinking?" asked Bonet.

"Yes, I invited a few friends to join us and then ordered another bottle of vodka for more shots. I thought it best to stick to that. I didn't want anyone being sick in my car."

Picard let out a nervous laugh and Bonet shot him a fierce look.

"Elaine loves dancing, I think she asked Xavier but he refused. I offered instead so we danced to a few tracks, leaving him at the table. When we got back, I had a quick shot then left them alone to talk to my other friends in the club," Jack explained.

"When did you notice that Monsieur de Verre had gone?" Bonet was certain almost everything he was saying was a truthful, yet slanted lie.

"I think maybe an hour or so, probably less. They had practically finished the bottle when I returned to the booth. Elaine was trying to sit on de Verre's lap, hanging onto him. She said something to him, I didn't hear what. He just pushed her roughly away, got up and walked off. We thought he was going to the bathroom so we went to dance, although I have to say she was falling all over the place."

"Then what happened?" Bonet prompted.

"We went back to the table and Xavier still hadn't returned. I sent her to the bar to look for him whilst I went to check the bathroom, but he wasn't there. On the way back, I asked Annie the receptionist if she had seen him, and she said he had already left. When I told Elaine at the bar, she was really upset and started crying. She said she was going after him; I tried to stop her, that he wasn't worth it. Just let the prick walk home, it would teach him a lesson, Mr Superstar. I told her I'd drive her home, but when I looked over five minutes later, she was gone."

"What did you do then, Monsieur Winter?"

"Nothing, I stayed. I spoke to my friend Christian

but I know lots of people there, inspector." Jack was super confident, like a man with an alibi. "I just thought let them get on with it, quite honestly I'd had enough of them both. If they wanted to walk about the countryside in the middle of the night that was their problem. I didn't want to get involved anymore."

"Weren't you worried something might happen to them? After all they were both very drunk and you were their driver," chastened Bonet.

"Inspector, they are neither children nor my responsibility." Jack was more than a match for him. "This is Lassay, nothing ever happens here. I assumed they would walk, hitch or find a friend."

"What time did you eventually leave the club?" asked Bonet.

"I can't tell you inspector, later than 3.00am, but I do remember it was light when I got into bed if that helps."

"Thank you, that is enough for now. We will need you to remember the names of anybody you spoke to that night, so we can confirm your statement and time of departure. By the way did you drive home, Monsieur Winter?"

"Yes inspector, I am ashamed to admit it. I know I shouldn't have, but there are not many taxis around here at night. I certainly wouldn't want to walk all that way." Even under these circumstances, he was smug.

"Then I would like to have the route you drove home please," added Bonet, so Jack told him and even offered to draw a map in Picard's notebook.

Jack Winter was a very cool customer indeed. He may not have been involved with this disappearance, but there was something very unsettling about him. He was far too calm and pleased with himself for someone who had just lost a friend and ex-lover.

His smirking face was that of a man who had got away with something, yet if not this crime, what else had he been up to? There was something about Jack Winter that made his teeth hurt. Bonet was rarely mistaken in his instincts.

Chapter 22

Catherine Segat was working late on Thursday night trying to finish a story on the ailing Airbus, when the first reports that something had happened in a little town called Lassay-les-Châteaux started coming in. Catherine had worked for the newspaper *Ouest-France* for the past two years and had proved herself a competent journalist. They had regional part-time reporters and photographers all over western France. Despite the hour, she immediately got on the phone to her editor at home to explain that a big story was breaking in her region and asked if she could cover it.

By 8.00am on Friday morning she had phoned ahead to reserve herself a room in the only hotel in Lassay, packed and researched her route from Nantes and was on her way. She arrived in Lassay before midday and parked at the back of the town hall. Local people had been gathering all day in the town square, standing in groups discussing the tragedy that had befallen the Dubois family.

Catherine immediately noticed that some

reporters were amongst them already gleaning information. She recognised her friend Martin Fouget who worked for Canal Plus already filming the scene. She had been at university in Nantes with Martin studying journalism. She waved to him as she crossed the square to the hotel, no doubt he was staying in the same place. She would check-in and then catch up with him to see what he had uncovered.

The hotel reception was packed with other journalists, and Catherine was pleased she had the foresight to phone and book first thing. She waited at the desk for the pale blonde woman scuttling around to get to her.

Jayne was very nervous working amongst so many French people, but luckily many of them tried to help her by speaking English. She noticed the young red-haired woman waiting with a large overnight bag on her shoulder.

"I have a reservation. It's for Catherine Segat, *Ouest-France*."

Jayne searched the list and found the name and allocated room number.

"Are you English, madame?" asked Catherine.

"Yes, sorry. My French is terrible," Jayne apologised, as usual.

"That's ok, I'm sure most of them can understand

you," said Catherine, indicating the other journalists waiting behind her.

"You had better hurry," Catherine advised.

"Thank you, I will," Jayne replied.

"I think they're all going to the social hall for the press briefing at 2.00pm. You will be full until we get our story. By the way, what is your name?" Catherine asked as an afterthought.

You never knew when it would come in handy to have made friends with the staff and other locals. They may well know things even the police and gendarmerie did not.

"I'm Jayne," she told her. "I'm just helping out whilst Jack takes care of some business."

"With the police?" Catherine asked.

Jayne said nothing and just looked at the floor.

"Is Jack the owner here, Jayne?" she tried another approach.

"No, not the owner. He runs this place for his uncle," she replied, handing over the bedroom key.

"Thank you very much," Catherine took the key and left. The woman had a queue, she could find her own way.

Catherine dumped her bag on the single bed, then went and splashed her face with cold water in the dated bathroom. She had stayed in worse hotels, many times. She dried her face on a clean rough towel then wandered over to the window facing out onto the town square. It was time for her to get down there and get her story.

There were small clusters of people gathered everywhere; some she recognised as journalists, but also locals whispering the story of a grisly murder in their town. They named and blamed the foreigners who should not be allowed to stay there for what had happened.

Everyone was gossiping and muttering about Xavier de Verre and his famous family. They were eager to repeat every detail about poor Nicolas Preton, who had still not recovered from finding Elaine the way he did.

Catherine followed the crowd up to the social hall to the official press conference and took a place next to Martin.

“Hi, how are you?” she said, kissing him on both cheeks.

“I’m great, loving Canal Plus. We’re trying to swing an interview with de Verre after this. You should tag along, see what you can get,” he said generously. They were old friends who went way back.

The room was buzzing as Inspector Bonet and Captain Gaston took their seats on the stage. The official line was unhelpful as usual, nothing to get excited about. They had little to share at present, no details or specifics. They were still awaiting the forensic report to verify the time and cause of death. They fielded the questions effortlessly, because they had few answers so early in the investigation.

When the meeting broke up less than an hour later, everyone was left to speculate as to what had really occurred. Catherine jumped into the back of Martin's Jeep and headed with several others to the de Verre house, unaware that this was within walking distance of the village.

Nobody could get near the protected house or its occupants. The gates were firmly locked with a gendarme outside. Martin wanted to stay close in case he could get some footage, so Catherine walked back to the hotel to start writing up her account of the official story.

Jayne was still running around although the place had cleared considerably. Catherine ordered a coffee and sat at one of the tables in the reception with her laptop, not wanting to be in her cramped little room any longer than necessary.

Her choice paid off as she was a few hundred words in, when Jack Winter came through the front door. He was handsome and very tall she noticed, as he walked straight over to catch up with Jayne. He then answered the phone and she realised he was completely fluent in French.

Jack had noticed the tidy redhead in the corner tapping away at her computer; not his type, but interesting all the same. He could tell she had a reasonable figure, but was not keen on the short red hair. Her clean good looks and slightly freckled pixie face were appealing.

Catherine tried to concentrate on her story, but her eyes strayed from the screen to Jack. He noticed her glancing at him, so he fixed his gaze on her until she looked over again, then gave her a blast of his dazzling smile. She flushed pink and Jack took it as a sign to approach her. He always enjoyed watching how women reacted to him, it gave him an enormous sense of power.

"I'm Jack Winter. I manage this hotel," he introduced himself, holding out his hand which she took.

Catherine managed to get her silly blush under control. She hated her pale skin that gave off so many involuntary signals. He deliberately squeezed her hand and held it longer than necessary.

"Catherine Segat," she responded, gently pulling her hand away. "I'm here to cover the story for *Ouest-France*."

"Yes, it's a terrible thing to happen in Lassay. I was with her you know, the night she disappeared.

I really wish she had accepted my offer of a lift home, then none of this would have happened," Jack confessed.

Catherine was excited, this was exactly the kind of exclusive she needed for her story. She had to find out who else he might have spoken to. Would he go on the record?

"Perhaps you would like to tell me about it over a drink later?" she asked boldly. It didn't pay to be too shy and retiring in her business.

"Why later?" he smiled invitingly, then went into the kitchen and produced a bottle of wine and two glasses.

"Would you like to come into my private office?"

Catherine was thrilled. This was a real break, damn right she would like to. She followed him whilst Jayne's haunted eyes watched them disappear.

Chapter 23

Inspector Giles Bonet left Lassay after the press briefing and headed home towards Rennes. He needed to pick up some things, as it looked likely he would have to stay in Lassay for the duration of the investigation. Since it was on his route, he was heading to the mortuary first and called Dr Jules Calvert before leaving.

It was vital that the doctor had established the cause of death. He would be able to send a copy of the initial report and make contact with the investigating judge, so they would be ready to issue any necessary warrants depending on the forensic results.

Dr Calvert met him in the reception of Mayenne Hospital and led him through the plain corridors to the mortuary. In that quiet, sterile space he opened the drawer containing Elaine Dubois. Bonet had seen many bodies, but this once young and beautiful woman so badly mangled was particularly unpleasant. It could be one of his daughters laid there.

The medical examiner started explaining what he

had found so far. With this level of decomposition, the time of death was impossible to determine until the samples returned from the laboratory, but the evidence suggested she had died at the scene on Monday morning.

There were contusions down her spine and significant bruising to both hips, made by human hands. The marks were large, and the placing was consistent with sexual activity. Elaine had experienced intercourse, both vaginal and anal, before her death. Most likely wearing a condom, as there was no trace of semen.

Her nose, mouth and upper trachea were blocked with earth and tree mulch, indicating her face had been pushed into the ground until she had stopped breathing. Probable cause of death was suffocation, not a broken neck or other injury. The mutilation was post-mortem, most likely inflicted by wild animals.

He had arranged for the body to be transported to his own department in Rennes, where he would be able to look at any fibres found and possible DNA traces.

"This is the preliminary report, Giles. I'm sure we can pick up more but it's very hard," Dr Calvert frowned. "Unfortunately, the ground around the body was destroyed by too many footprints. We're still sifting through the samples taken from the site, but as yet we have nothing."

"Still no trace of the mobile phone or handbag?" Bonet asked.

"No."

"Thank you, Jules, I appreciate you helping out with this one. Keep me posted concerning fibres or DNA but this should be enough to get a warrant. I'm nipping home to scrub up and then back to Lassay. I'll give you a call tomorrow at the lab and see if you have anything else." Bonet shook the doctor's hand and went back to his car.

This investigation was getting more difficult over time. With limited forensic proof, it would be hard to place de Verre or Winter at the scene of the crime. Considering Elaine had spent the previous night with both of them, any of their clothing fibres found on her body could have been picked up during the course of the evening.

Maybe the finger marks on her hips? Jack in particular was clearly very big and likely to be strong, but the fact that the bruises had been made by large hands was nothing really to go on. Almost any man was capable of causing that kind of harm, his own hands could have inflicted those marks. Could this be an accidental death from rough but consensual sex?

As he drove along smoking, something that Jules had said kept bothering him. There were no signs of semen and the perpetrator had most likely worn a condom. Did a man as drunk as de Verre have the forethought to glove up? On the other hand, he had managed to find his way home in an area unknown to him, so maybe he wasn't as drunk as he said he was.

Jack had also claimed not to have drunk as much as the other two, but he could be lying to cover his driving infractions. With her mobile phone and bag unaccounted for, Bonet wanted to search Jack Winter's vehicle.

He would talk to his commander and confirm who was the assigned investigating judge. He had been waiting until he had something substantial, but he could get emergency warrants issued tonight based on the preliminary forensic report to search the car and gather clothing from the suspects.

Bonet had not as yet contacted the family directly, but was informed by his commander, who had spoken with Jean de Verre, that Yvette de Verre-Müller and an English socialite called Lady Victoria de Savory were both inside de Verre's residence. The solicitor would be there for a formal interview at noon tomorrow.

He had a nasty feeling about this whole case. The amount of media attention would be a real problem and the locals were already upset. The two well-known suspects were both outsiders, obvious and high-profile in town, and it could lead to vigilantes taking things into their own hands.

He had noted that Jean de Verre had brought in his own security to guard his son's home and at his request, the gendarme was placed outside the gate.

Things were escalating rapidly and it would be difficult to contain. There were at least twenty reporters at the press briefing and who knew how many more on their way. The hotel was already full, but they would sleep in their vans if necessary or bribe locals for a room. All this for a photo or a story, some unique take on the terrible grief, pain and suffering of a family and community.

Bonet called Lieutenant Picard and arranged for him to collect the evidence from the hotel early tomorrow morning. He would take him along to the interview with Xavier de Verre and his solicitor later.

He was glad to have Picard on board, he was proving invaluable for his local knowledge. Even Officer Arnaud had volunteered to go back and guard his chief tonight and he appreciated their loyalty at this time of personal crisis for him. Bonet himself needed to get back before causing any more trouble of his own. His wife would be mad, he needed to retire before that woman nagged him to death.

Chapter 24

Catherine was glad to get back to her room to consider the last hour she had spent with the handsome Jack Winter. Catherine was not the young girl she resembled; she was extremely intuitive and very quickly during the conversation, she picked up that there was something in Jack's story that sounded malicious. She did not understand why he wanted to implicate Xavier de Verre so badly. To hide his own guilt?

Perhaps it was just jealousy because de Verre was famous and represented some very serious competition. There was definitely more digging to do here. She could feel that she was on the right track to finding out what had really happened that night. In the meantime, she would wash up and go to the Víctor pub and listen to the local gossip.

Jack felt pleased with his interview with Catherine. He knew that she fancied him, most women did, and he'd had her soaking up his story about that fateful night. The drunken revelry of the evening and the way Elaine had thrown herself at a man clearly not interested. Catherine lapped up every juicy detail he laid out for her; he considered it foreplay and was very much looking forward to seeing her again.

Most of the journalists had gone in search of supper in the local pizza place, so he had time to check up on Jayne and see if she had finished work and needed paying. He sauntered into the kitchen.

“How are you doing beautiful? I just wanted to say that you have been amazing today. I don’t know what I would have done without you.”

“It’s quiet now and I have a bottle of champagne on ice, especially to say thank you sweetheart.” He flashed her a winning smile as he slipped two fifty euro notes into her rough hand.

“Thanks Jack, that’s kind of you but I should get home. I’m really tired and I expect you will need me again tomorrow?”

“Yes darling, I will never not need you at the moment. I can’t cope with all these journalists alone, you know that. This is your chance to earn some proper money to help your situation. You know I understand how hard it is for you. I’ve seen your house,” Jack winked, as if he were completely innocent of any wrongdoing.

Jayne knew she shouldn’t stay after the way he had treated her last time. It was true he had not forced her, well not exactly. Did she even try and say no or stop it? Had he actually harmed her? Degraded her, yes. He was very drunk, perhaps he was unaware of what he had done. Or worse, didn't see anything wrong with that kind of behaviour?

These nagging thoughts were influencing her, as she talked herself into the necessary acceptance. Standing in front of her smiling, she forgot the inconsiderate brute of the other night and just saw his handsome face. He was charm personified and more importantly, he was there.

She was really very lonely and had been for a long time. She had nobody to go home to. Her husband hadn't spoken to her for more than two weeks, nor replied to any calls or messages. The truth had started to sink in and she knew now that she had been abandoned. Could it be different this time with Jack? Could they start over with a clean slate?

"Ok, but only one glass then I must go," she decided, hating herself yet still pathetically grateful for the company, the attention, the human contact.

Jack took her work-worn hands in his and kissed each finger, looking into her eyes. With deep sincerity he told her how beautiful he found her, how he admired her strength to survive, and how he understood the difficulties she faced and only wanted to help.

What salve he provided to a rejected and broken

woman, not old enough to have forgotten what it felt like to be loved and wanted. It was all too familiar and such easy pickings for a scoundrel like Jack, a modern-day Lothario when it came to seduction. He collected the champagne on ice and a couple of flutes as he gently steered her to his private room.

***

Jayne crept out from under Jack's heavy arm, which had held her pinned down until he fell asleep. She crawled out of the bed and realised as she stood up how much she hurt. Jack had bitten her in a frenzied attack on her body. He had clamped his hand over her mouth.

"Shush Jayne, no noise," he said, looking into her eyes.

She had been absolutely terrified. He had started off so gentle and caring. They had shared the champagne and congratulated each other on good teamwork, although in reality Jayne had done most of the work.

Gradually his charm and compliments had her undressed and on her back. What started as normal love-making soon changed. After a few minutes he called her Alex by mistake, which made him angry and he switched. Suddenly he was filled with rage and pounding into her, really trying to hurt her each time he slammed against her.

“I know what you’ve been up to Alex, you dirty bitch.”

He was raving on about what she had done in the hotel that night. He had a camera in the room and it was all on film, so no need to deny it.

“I saw you fucking all those men, you whore. This is what you deserve Alex, I’m going to punish you.”

He continued pounding her and then before his climax started going wild, clawing and biting at her in a frenzy. She screamed out in pain as his teeth tore at her breasts. He was a mad-man, possessed and overcome. It was like his sanity slipped, he totally believed she was this Alex woman and she thought he was going to kill her.

As soon as she could escape, Jayne rushed home and threw herself into a hot shower. Her breasts were covered with bites, there was no back-tracking this time. It was perfectly evident, she had definitely been seriously assaulted. Was she only alive because he needed her to look after his guests and to clean his hotel?

Suddenly she realised Jack was with Elaine the night she died, and after her experience, thought she knew exactly what had happened to her. But what was all that crazy business about Alex? Who was she? Jayne had to tell someone the truth, she had to confess her dark secret. She was certain Jack had killed Elaine Dubois when his rough sex had become uncontrollable.

***

Catherine awoke early and went to open the window of her stuffy room. She immediately noticed the gendarmerie vehicle parked outside. She dressed quickly and hurried downstairs, where she saw several gendarmes and Jack waiting in the reception. She discreetly stood watching from the kitchen doorway, making herself invisible.

Within a few moments Jayne arrived, flushed and rushing, as if she had been urgently summoned. The gendarmes stood up and escorted Jack towards the door, but when he drew close to her, he stopped and gave instructions.

"Keep it all under control until I get back. Overtime pay of course," he added, sneering and daring her to refuse him.

Jack was then ushered into the waiting vehicle by Lieutenant Picard.

The investigating judge had issued the warrants last night and the search of Jack's car had turned up some very interesting evidence indeed. A pair of black high-heeled shoes had been discovered under the passenger seat that matched the statement of Annie, the receptionist of La Pellu.

Picard had remembered her description of Elaine's high heels and skimpy dress from when the girl came past her drunkenly crying and stumbling into the night. It felt good to be able to detain Winter and he was longing to use his cuffs, but he'd come willingly as if he was without a care in the world.

Catherine took a seat at the window table in the foyer, watching as this scene unfolded. After the last gendarme pulled away, she wandered back towards the kitchen to see if she could get a coffee and find out what had happened from Jayne.

Jayne was there, but when she turned startled, Catherine saw her face and Jayne burst into tears. Catherine instinctively put her arms around the shaking woman's shoulders and tried to dig up her best English, much harder in a crisis.

"For God's sake! Let me look at you," Catherine insisted, turning to examine her puffy tear-stained face. There was a vicious mark on her neck.

"Jayne, what happened to you?"

Jayne lifted up her top and showed Catherine her breasts, which were too painful for her to wear a bra. They were covered with bruises and what could only be small wounds from bites.

"You must report this." Catherine was horrified.

"Was it Jack?"

Jayne nodded her reply.

"*Mon dieu*!" she crossed herself. "Is that why the gendarmes were here?"

"No, I haven't told anyone. They just called me and asked me to come in and cover immediately."

"Do you think he killed Elaine Dubois?" Catherine pressed.

Jayne was mute. How could she accuse someone if she was not certain?

"Jayne, answer me!" she demanded.

"Yes! Yes!" Jayne finally cried out, covering her face with her hands.

"I was so frightened," she went on. "It's all I kept thinking, but I went to his room willingly! What kind of fool am I?"

"Don't think like that!" Catherine shouted back at her, angry with her and for her. "You cannot take the blame for this. He is a monster. Did you want him to do this to you? No!"

Jayne sobbed in her arms. Catherine gave her half a minute to gather herself, before offering her some napkins.

"Here."

Jayne reached out to take them, but Catherine caught her hand and held her eyes.

"Jayne, you must tell the gendarmerie. You know that?"

There was a tapping on the kitchen door and Jayne rushed past Catherine to see to another guest. Catherine let her go, for now. What a story she was on to, but her heart went out to the traumatised woman. She would help strengthen her, give her some resolve to push forward and do the right thing.

The foyer had started to fill up with journalists wanting coffee and a good wi-fi connection. Jayne got busy running around filling orders and Catherine reclaimed her window seat, but every now and then she caught Jayne's eye and gave her a reassuring nod. A rumour spread that the solicitor for the de Verre family had arrived and there would be a statement for the press, so everyone left like a shoal of fish.

Jayne was just clearing the coffee cups away when a tall blonde woman came in and waited at the desk. She was wearing jeans and a t-shirt but making them look special, helped by her very large, Jackie-style sunglasses. Jayne didn't think she looked French, so asked her in English how she could help.

"I'm looking for Jack," she replied. "My name is

Alex Taylor."

Jayne froze, she just knew that this was the Alex that Jack had been punishing last night. Catherine noticed the look on Jayne's face and came over immediately. She introduced herself, but Alex didn't want to speak to the press. She only came to find out from Jack what was going on, as she had heard nothing from Xavier.

Catherine ushered all the women into the kitchen. Before anybody could say anything, she got straight to the point.

"Show Alex, she needs to know," she said to Jayne.

Jayne reluctantly lifted her top again to reveal her tender, wounded breasts.

"What's this?" Alex was appalled at the sight.

"Jack," said Catherine, not concealing her horror.

The second longer glimpse in bright lighting confirmed the extent of what she had suffered. He had ravaged her and she was badly bruised and covered in wounds where his teeth had punctured her pale skin. All three women looked at each other. This had to be reported, immediately.

Chapter 25

Picard had called Bonet when the search had revealed the shoes in Jack Winter's car. He had confirmed to detain him for further questioning. The forensic evidence had been collected along with the suspect, who was on his way to the gendarmerie headquarters. He was to be left to cool down at the station until he got there later, let the games begin.

The interview with Xavier de Verre would be conducted in his home with his solicitor present. The family intended to make a statement afterwards to the press. This was a stressful situation but they had experience with such things. Bonet would handle the formal interview very carefully and respectful of the family's status and position.

Nobody was more unpleasantly surprised than Inspector Giles Bonet, when he arrived at the gendarmerie in Lassay to collect Picard, to find Captain Charles Dubois in uniform and in his office. He had no time to deal with this before the interview, so left an urgent message for the deputy chief to keep an eye on him, or assign an officer to watch him, or better still, persuade him to go home.

“What do you make of the chief?” Picard asked him, when he met Bonet at the car.

“I don’t want him getting involved,” Bonet confirmed the obvious. “He cannot be part of this investigation. He needs to be with his family to grieve in private.”

Picard was silent. Clearly he had something else on his mind, but Bonet was patient. The young man would speak when he had something to say.

“Inspector, the local hunt was out on Monday morning at 4.00am. I spoke to young Nicolas Preton, the one who found Elaine’s body. He’s very cut up about it, he thinks he could have saved her,” Picard told him. “According to him, his truck had broken down near to where Elaine was found. He called Jacques Legrand who lives on that route to collect him on his way, but Legrand didn’t show up before another member of his hunting group came past and picked him up. He never thought anything of it.”

“Who is Jacques Legrand?”

“Sophie Dubois, Elaine’s sister, is actually Sophie Legrand. Jacques is her husband.”

“Where was Legrand when Nicolas Preton called

him? Did he make it to the hunt?" Bonet asked and Picard shrugged his shoulders, indicating he knew no more.

Someone else was driving around the exact place that Elaine had disappeared? In fact, potentially many of the nearby village men Bonet realised. He would have to round up and interview the members of the local hunt if they were out and about in the countryside. They may have seen or heard something without noticing the significance. This case was getting bigger by the day and he needed a breakthrough. His wife would be furious, but what could he do?

They pulled up in front of the de Verre house, noticing the gendarme still stationed outside. There was also a crowd of journalists gathering and talking amongst themselves. The gates were opened by the private security guards to allow the officers onto the semi-circular drive.

They were met at the door by another armed security guard and shown into the exquisite 18th century drawing room. Xavier, his mother and their solicitor were seated. Inspector Bonet was not going to publicly advertise their previous connection unless the family chose to themselves. He conducted himself with perfect formality due to the seriousness of the investigation.

Bonet went straight to Yvette de Verre, a brief meeting of eyes showing mutual recognition, as he officially introduced himself and the lieutenant. She was still a great beauty and every bit the model of elegance.

"Please excuse me, Madame de Verre, but I have to ask you to leave."

"It's Müller now," Yvette smiled at the inspector who she knew well, although it had been many years since she had seen him.

"Of course," Giles nodded respectfully. "This is now a criminal investigation. Please be assured we are doing everything to expedite this process, to save your family further embarrassment."

The solicitor Maître Honoré gently ushered Yvette into the conservatory where Victoria was waiting. She would have her moment soon on the steps of her son's home, with a carefully prepared statement from the family announcing their son's innocence. They would give the investigation their full co-operation and were praying for the family of the unfortunate girl. After which she would thank the press for their support and ask them to respect their privacy.

It was another hour before Bonet and Picard left. The formal interview had been disappointing, but he was no longer their prime suspect with Winter in custody. With his solicitor present, Xavier de Verre had been extremely cautious in his replies and they had learnt little that they did not already know. They collected the clothes Xavier had been wearing as a formality, and took down his vehicle details before they drove swiftly away.

As they departed, Yvette watched through the drawing room window. She could see the cameras flashing as the gates opened to let them out. Soon it would be time for the circus to begin and she would play her part to perfection.

***

Bonet and Picard went straight to the interview room where Jack was waiting. He sat slumped over the table with his head resting on his arms as though sleeping, yet it was obvious that he was awake. Picard set up the recording and this time they confirmed his rights and asked if he was happy to proceed without a solicitor.

“Of course, I’m not guilty,” he answered cockily. “Why would I need a lawyer?”

Bonet went through his previous statement again. He answered confidently and consistently, but something didn’t feel right. Jack sounded rehearsed rather than real, and was altogether too glib for a man who still had the issue of the time unaccounted for, when he claimed to be driving home alone.

“So you never saw Elaine again after you left the club?”

"I drove straight home. I gave you my route but there must be lots of people who can confirm I stayed on. Did you speak to Christian?"

"I ask the questions." Bonet decided to give him a jolt. "Earlier we took a pair of black high-heeled shoes from under the passenger seat of your car, Monsieur Winter. How do you explain that?"

"I don't wear high heels, inspector."

"The shoes match a description given by a witness as belonging to Elaine Dubois."

"Elaine has been in my car several times," Jack replied calmly. "So have many other women who may or may not have forgotten their shoes. What size are they and maybe I can identify the lady in question?"

"How could the shoes the victim was wearing that night find their way into your car?" Bonet wasn't going to let him off so easily.

"Maybe she went to my car to wait for me, I never leave it locked. I stayed at least an hour later, perhaps she got fed up waiting and walked off without them."

"Barefoot into the night?" Bonet was incredulous.

"Clearly you don't have much experience of drunken young women and their tantrums," he replied smoothly.

Jack had an answer for everything and this interview was going nowhere. Since the shoes were now a crucial piece of evidence, this gave them the grounds to detain Jack for further questioning. They would need to bring in Annie the receptionist to look at the evidence and see if she could identify them as Elaine's, before disturbing her family.

Bonet knew that this was no conclusive evidence of guilt. Most probably a guilty man would have checked and made sure to get rid of such items right away, but it was enough to keep Jack Winter under lock and key as long as the law allowed.

***

After making little headway with Jack, Inspector Giles Bonet took a break. He made a call and updated his commander in Rennes, who congratulated him on his progress and for handling de Verre carefully. Both men were relieved that he was the least likely suspect, now they had potential evidence against Winter.

Bonet put the phone down. He badly wanted a cigarette, but instinctively reached for his moustache instead. He went to look for Picard.

"Come with me to the car," he instructed. "Leave Winter to sit and stew for a few hours. He is officially our prime suspect, but until then, I want to track down the hunt and follow up on the whereabouts of Jacques Legrand."

Chapter 26

Alex wanted them all to go straight to the gendarmerie headquarters. Catherine would have to escort Jayne to translate, but it was too important to conceal what Jack had done to her. They were holding him now, but they may let him go if they did not speak up. Alex was sure that he had killed Elaine. Jayne had obviously been through a terrible ordeal; she could only imagine what she had experienced. Yet Alex could not forget that she had slept with that psychopath willingly.

Alex was frightened but she had to give her own evidence against Jack, she couldn't let it happen to another woman. Jayne had not told Alex that he had called out her name whilst he assaulted her. Catherine knew neither woman spoke enough French to make their experiences count, and was pleased to be able to support them. Her story had just become more fantastic than she could have hoped, an amazing exclusive that would distinguish her from all the others.

When Captain Dubois heard that there were three

women in the station wanting to talk to somebody about Jack Winter, he took advantage of Bonet's absence and gave instructions to have them brought to him.

Charles had observed Winter through the window of the interview room but had not gone in. He had seen him in town swaggering around pretending to be French, chatting to all the women. He knew he was just the type his sister would have gone for and probably had done. Could that bastard Winter be responsible? Dubois was certain he was capable of it; he was a nasty piece of work beneath the veneer of charm and good looks.

The chief politely offered the women seats in a larger interview room and asked how he could assist them. He was shocked when they disclosed their story. Catherine Segat could only say so much, before Jayne Slater raised her top to show evident physical assault.

As she revealed the bite marks on her chest and neck, he was truly horrified. Jayne went on and briefly told him about the attack. Alex started to add her contributions of the strange behaviour and accusations she had experienced.

The chief halted them. He would have to take a formal statement from them and would need another officer. He asked them all to take a seat in the reception, and assured them he would not be long.

Charles calmly returned to his office, opened his desk drawer and took out his service pistol, making sure it had only one bullet. He walked into the room where Jack Winter was being held. He went up to him and instantly shot him in the head. Then all hell broke loose.

***

The chief was immobile; he sat on the chair opposite the dead man with un-seeing eyes, whilst colleagues stood stunned looking through the doorway at this real-life tragedy, right in front of them.

Catherine heard the gunshot. It seemed to reverberate around the building. She quickly slipped through the doorway to the crowded hallway to see them now guiding the chief along the corridor. He was pale and clearly in shock, but was allowing himself to be led.

Catherine took advantage to creep even closer, as she looked past the crowd clustered around the doorway, she saw the dead body of Jack Winter, shot by the grieving brother of Elaine Dubois.

He was sprawled on a chair, his head thrown back in a comical, scarecrow-like stance. The bullet had blown to pieces a quarter of his skull. Catherine whipped out her phone surreptitiously.

The Confession

Bonet and Picard turned their car into an empty yard, only a pick-up truck sitting in the corner. There were dogs barking somewhere, maybe tied up in the barn. They had made several calls and confirmed that Jacques did not turn up for Nicolas Preton when he was broken down. Nicolas had hitched a lift to the hunt with others, none of whom could remember Jacques arriving at all.

They knocked on the small farmhouse door but there was no reply, so Picard walked over and looked through the window. Jacques was sitting at the kitchen table with his shotgun in front of him. His face had the look of a desperate man.

Picard knocked gently on the window and called out to him.

"Open the door Jacques, we would like to talk to you."

Jacques did not look surprised, he just stood up and indicated the front door. Picard found it unlocked, so he entered with Bonet and together they went into the country kitchen. Jacques had returned to his seat in front of his shotgun.

"You don't need that, Jacques," Picard pointed to the gun.

"Can we sit down and talk to you? About the night Elaine disappeared and where you were?" Bonet continued.

Jacques offered them some of his own armagnac, but they both refused as they were on duty. They took seats at the table and looked into the eyes of a man carrying a huge burden, he knew there was nowhere to go. He did not look dangerous, considering the presumably loaded shotgun in front of him; it was pure despair that registered on his face.

"Tell us what happened," Bonet said simply.

"I got her call minutes after Nicolas phoned me," Jacques started. "I was already on my way out anyway to join the hunt. Instead of collecting Nicolas, I picked her up along the road outside La Pellu."

"Then what?" Picard prompted.

"I knew she had made a fool of herself with that Xavier de Verre. She was drunk and hysterical, begging me to come and get her. She was crying on the phone that she had been a very bad girl. That was our sign, I knew she wanted me so we drove to the wood," he stopped. It was all coming out now.

"It wasn't the first time, inspector. We'd done it many times, since before I was married; but we carried on whenever she needed me to punish her. That was our game, our excuse. We both wanted the excitement, but it went too far!"

Jacques dropped his head into his hands.

"Secrets, inspector, dark secrets. Sophie knows."

"What makes you say that, Jacques?" asked Bonet gently.

"When I got up this morning, she had my phone in her hand," Jacques explained. "She must have gone through it and seen Elaine's call. She just looked at me, took the children, got in her car and drove away. I assume to the house of her parents, or maybe her wonderful brother, hence you are here?"

"Jacques we will have to take you to the station, you know that don't you?" Bonet stood up. Jacques simply nodded his head.

Jacques looked around his kitchen, nothing could ever be the same again. His life was over and everyone would know, he should have just shot himself and saved his family the shame. A broken man walked to the police vehicle and meekly got in.

Jacques was silent in the back of the car. Picard

knew him from college, although he was a few years older. He understood what had driven him to play this dangerous game with Elaine. Picard had also known her intimately, like most of the virile males in a small town. It was definitely time to leave, he reflected. He would speak to the chief, get him to give him a recommendation. Perhaps Bonet could advise him on his career path.

It was pandemonium at the station. The gates at the front of the gendarmerie had been shut, and the press were blocking them and had spilled out along the main road. There was a baying crowd outside the gates, but they managed to get through into the back of the main compound, past reporters and film crews already in town following the story.

"What's going on here?" shouted Bonet to the first officer he came to.

"Sir, it's the chief. He's shot the suspect!" The young gendarme looked gobsmacked.

They thrust Jacques into the nearest holding cell and ordered another gendarme to stay with him.

"Do not let him out of your sight," thundered Bonet, desperate to record his statement.

Bonet and Picard rushed through to the reception.

"What exactly happened before the chief shot the suspect?" Bonet demanded of the desk officer.

"The chief was interviewing those people over there," he pointed.

The three women were seated, huddled together looking shaken. A female gendarme was talking to them.

"Where is the chief now?" Picard asked.

"In his office," he replied, another white face and haunted look.

Bonet rushed down the corridor and on his way, saw the lifeless form of Jack Winter who was clearly dead.

"He's been shot in the head. It would have been instant," the leading paramedic confirmed. "We haven't touched him, we'll leave everything for forensics."

Bonet felt Picard at his elbow and together they walked towards the office. It was time to tell another broken man the worst possible news. This dark secret would destroy his family, his career, his life.

Captain Dubois sat in the office, upright in his pristine uniform, composed and silently staring.

"Charles, can you hear me?" Dubois didn't move or alter his faraway focus.

"He's been like this since we arrived. He hasn't

said a word, nothing at all," one of the paramedics informed them. "We have tried but there is no reaction."

Clearly the chief was in need of psychiatric care. Bonet had seen this sort of psychotic episode before. It may be days before he was lucid and aware, if indeed he ever recovered. He needed to know what those three women had said to Captain Dubois.

Bonet sent Picard off to collect them from reception. None of these people had featured in his investigation so far, but they clearly held the answers to slot together the final pieces of the puzzle.

Bonet set up and started the tape recorder, aware Jacques Legrand was waiting. The confession was exactly what he needed to close this case and exonerate Xavier de Verre. Captain Charles Dubois had killed the wrong man, an innocent man. It was unbelievable the turn of events, yet there was more to come.

Catherine Segat immediately introduced herself and explained that the others spoke little French. She was a journalist staying at the hotel in town and they had come to report a crime.

Bonet was surprised when Picard interrupted and asked in excellent English for the names and details from Alex and Jayne. Once the formalities were complete and the identities established, everything was on the record and Catherine began the sorry tale.

After Jack was taken away by the gendarmes that morning, she had seen Jayne crying. When she went over to comfort her, she had spotted a mark on Jayne's neck and asked what happened. Jayne had told her that Jack had attacked her.

Bonet could see the mark on her neck that was being referred to. Upon his request, she stood up and lifted her top to show the other bites lower down. Bonet grimaced, the poor woman. Jayne was clearly traumatised.

"Jayne, in your own words, what happened to you?"

"It was Jack Winter," Jayne spoke up, pausing between sentences so Catherine could translate. "The first time, it was sort of voluntary when he forced himself on me. I thought it was my fault, I was just going to leave. I had no choice, no money, nothing. My husband has gone. I am just stranded here with debts and a house that is falling down. Jack was exciting, I thought he really liked me, he bought me champagne!" she started sobbing again.

"How exactly did you get all these wounds?" Bonet steered her back on course.

"He attacked me last night in his room at the hotel.

I know he was out that night with Elaine Dubois and I had to tell somebody the truth."

Jayne broke down again and Alex leant across with a tissue for her, before starting her account.

"Inspector, we wanted to report this before they let Jack go." Alex also waited so Catherine could translate. "Jayne has obviously been abused and I have experienced bizarre and aggressive behaviour from Jack."

"Can you be more specific?" Bonet enquired.

"Just the way he turned up at my house uninvited all the time. The things he said when I bumped into him in the street. Like he knew what I was doing in his hotel, that he had a video camera recording of me having sex with men," she revealed.

"Did you know what he was talking about?"

"Of course not!" Alex returned. "I was baffled, but I didn't forget it. It was sort of rambling, accusatory and almost unhinged. I was freaked out by the whole exchange and swore at him and told him to leave me alone. He had completely lost the plot."

"He called your name last night. While he was doing this to me," Jayne spoke up in a very quiet voice.

"When Jack attacked you, he called out the name of

Alex?" Picard asked in English and Bonet frowned.

"Yes, he said it more than once," Jayne replied immediately. "It took a long time what he did to me."

Jayne looked down at her hands in her lap and scrunched them into fists. She could not help feeling she had brought this whole nightmare on herself.

"He shouted at me 'you bitch Alex, I'll show you what you deserve'. Then he bit me some more as he raped me." Jayne was utterly authentic in her recounting of the ordeal.

Alex was pale, she had no idea how close she had come to being attacked at best and murdered at worst. She had slept with this man voluntarily and it had been the best sex of her life. This was a seriously disturbing thought. She had literally danced with the devil and survived to tell the tale. She was a very lucky girl who had escaped almost scot-free from an ordeal that had already killed one woman and horrifically damaged another.

"You told this to the chief, Captain Dubois?" Bonet pressed. "You showed him the bites?

The three women nodded. Bonet stopped the recording.

"We will take a break for ten minutes," Bonet said, getting up and heading for the door.

"Do you need a coffee or maybe we can make reasonable tea for your English tastes?" Picard asked, keen to show off his language skills.

Outside Bonet asked Picard to confirm the obvious.

"What do you think?"

"The chief heard their confession, deduced Jack Winter had killed his sister. Knowing he could never recover, hating him and wanting revenge, he decided to enact swift justice. A crime of passion if ever there was one," Picard added.

"Yes, I think you are right," reflected Bonet.

Chapter 27

When Catherine, Alex and Jayne were finally allowed to leave the station, Catherine drove them all back to the hotel. They needed a stiff drink to process the events of the day. Jayne went to the wine rack and pulled a bottle of merlot. She returned with three glasses and sat down in the reception with the others.

"I don't know what I'm supposed to do now? What about this place?" Jayne asked.

"It's not your responsibility," Alex protested. "You can't be expected to take care of it."

"Do you even know Jack, really? His uncle is clearly not very involved. Do you think we could find a number?" Catherine was always chasing details for her story.

"I'm going to leave just as soon as I can," Alex told Jayne. "You are quite welcome to come with me as far as London, if that helps?"

Jayne wasn't sure what to do. If she could stay on at the hotel, she may be able to salvage something of her life. She thanked Alex but told her she would wait to see what happened.

Catherine was itching to get on with her article, she was aware of just how much this would push her career forward if she could get it in first. She finished a glass of wine and looked at these two women, both victims of the terrible and tragic Jack Winter. She could see that they were survivors.

"I have to go and write ladies, that is my job; a story of jealousy and guilt, tragedy and secrets."

Catherine stood and shook hands in the English way.

"I hope it goes well for you both," she said sincerely. "If you don't mind, may I use some of your experiences to illustrate my piece?"

Jayne gave her permission, but Alex asked to remain anonymous.

"I am going Jayne, but please think about my offer," Alex insisted. "This is not a good place for you."

"I will Alex," Jayne tried to reassure her.

Alex drove past Xavier's home on the way back to her parents' house. It looked completely closed off; no press, no guards, shutters closed on the house. They would have been notified, of course. Xavier was off the hook and had left as soon as possible by the look of things. What could she have expected?

The strange attraction that she was sure they

had both felt was forever buried beneath the nightmare that had occurred in Lassay. Alex had been told she could go home. If they needed any further information, they would contact her directly. She went online and booked her ticket for the very next day.

Alex slept badly and was glad when it was time to leave. It was a gloomy morning and that seemed fitting after what had happened. She thought about her future as she drove through the French countryside. It was a new version of herself that was returning home. Things would be different, she was certain. She was taking back control of her life.

***

Inspector Giles Bonet had completed his report in his office in Rennes. He had been glad to get back to his own bed and his wife's cooking. Picard and his wife had been the kindest hosts, but home was home. He had cited Lieutenant Picard for a commendation for his work in Lassay. It had been his insight into the local people that had really cracked the case. A few comments that had slipped from Picard indicated that he also knew Elaine Dubois a little too well.

Bonet could not guess how the courts would treat Jacques Legrand. It had been an accident, certainly a crime of passion. During his recorded confession, he admitted to throwing Elaine's mobile phone and bag from his truck on the way home. Later he had found her shoes underneath the seat and attempted to get rid of the evidence, planting them in Jack's car to lay the blame elsewhere. Whatever his sentence, his life was over, his family gone, his farm left untended.

Before Bonet had left Lassay, he had called Xavier de Verre and told him that he was free to leave, although he may need to contact him in the future. Xavier had never felt so relieved. He didn't ask questions, just thanked the inspector and told his mother and Victoria.

"Thank God, darling! I'll call your father and let him know."

Within half an hour a helicopter arrived and took them away. They would go to Paris for a few days then disappear for several weeks and let the dust settle. Xavier thought about contacting Alex but when he went to make the call, he didn't know what to say so he left it. He thought maybe he would call in a few days, but he didn't.

Epilogue

London was grey today and raining lightly. The autumn colours were long gone and it was now the winter gloom of December. Alex had managed to get away from work early. She had left the office to pick up the District Line underground to Putney where she had rented a little Victorian cottage near the river Thames. She got a seat on the train, a luxury, and checked her phone. She had been talking to John recently, he was missing her and she had to really think about everything. At last, he was offering her more commitment.

Her phone showed a call from an unknown number. She had heard nothing from France since she had left, but considered that a good thing. She had read the story that Catherine had written. Jayne had stayed on at the hotel and was slowly re-building her life. Poor Elaine, and poor Jack in the end. He may have been a monster, but he was sick and clearly needed help. Then she had done her best to forget all about her nightmare holiday, and how close she had come to tragedy.

She hung up her raincoat in the small hallway,

kicked off her wet shoes and went to make a cup of tea. She had just left the kitchen when her phone rang. She saw the unknown number come up again and rushed to answer.

“Hello?”

“Alex?”

She knew his voice, the deep French tones. Her heart started pounding immediately, thumping in her chest.

“Xavier?”

“I didn’t know if you would talk to me? I’m in London,” he told her.

It took her a second to understand that he was there and he was calling her. She felt sick and elated at the same time.

“How are you doing? How come you’re here?”

“I hoped to see you. Can we meet?” Xavier asked directly.

There was silence as Alex hesitated.

“How about dinner? Somewhere near to you maybe?” he pressed.

“When?” Alex quickly racked her brains for a venue.

“Are you free tonight? I’m not in town long.”

Alex suggested El Cordoba, a small Spanish tapas bar two minutes from her door.

"That would be great, can we say 7.00pm?"

"Ok," she replied.

"I can't wait to see you, Alex," he said, his voice riddled with undertones. "There is so much we need to talk about. I'll be there." Xavier hung up the phone.

That gave Alex less than an hour to get herself together. She rummaged through her wardrobe for the right thing to wear and discarded everything. She eventually chose a dark emerald green, cross-over jersey dress that she had been saving for a special occasion. She showered and changed, spritzed herself with her favourite perfume and looked in the mirror.

Today she would be in charge, no messing around. She had moved on and was not in the same emotionally vulnerable position that she had been in last summer. She would drink little, eat something and behave like an adult.

El Cordoba was warm and cosy. Alex arrived early and asked for a table for two in the back area where they were quiet. She slipped into the candle-lit banquette the waitress showed her to. She told her that she was meeting somebody, then ordered a large glass of chablis and waited.

Soon it was 7.30pm and Alex felt like a fool. She had finished her wine and ordered another glass, thinking why not? He was clearly messing her around again! She was just deciding to get the bill and leave when he was there in front of her. He was soaking wet, shaking out his dark hair as he wiped the rain from his tanned face. He gave a perfect smile and apologised for being so late, as he couldn't find a taxi in the terrible weather.

They both stood awkwardly facing each other. Xavier moved towards her to kiss her cheeks in the traditional French way, and Alex felt her face burning red. She noticed over his shoulder the waitress looking at him, everyone there was looking at him. He really was the most beautiful man.

"How have you been?" he asked, taking a seat opposite her.

"Good thanks," Alex replied.

She was as dazzled in his presence as she always was. It took a while to get used to being this close to him again. Xavier looked wonderful, so handsome and vibrant. He was tanned and wearing a white linen shirt under his dark cashmere jacket which made him look so European. His hair was longer and looked kind of curly from the rain. He ordered a bottle of chablis and managed to make the waitress blush when he looked at her.

"Let's take a look at what you have," he said, checking the menu she handed him.

Xavier may have been hungry, but Alex doubted that she would be able to eat a thing. She let the waitress fill up her wine before saying that a mixed tapas would be fine. She had ordered it a few weeks ago with John in this very seat, she realised with a jolt.

"I'll have the same."

Xavier lifted his glass to hers with a tiny clink.

"To you, to me and maybe more," he toasted.

"I have drunk too much again. It seems to be the story of my relationship with you, Xav."

"I have a lot to apologise for Alex. I think it's easier if you have drunk too much. I wanted to call you, I wanted to so many times but I couldn't," he went on. "I didn't know what to say, or if you would even want to speak to me after Lassay. Elaine was dead, then Jack was dead. So much had happened so fast, the whole sordid business, and then you, one minute you were there and the next gone. My family just wanted to get me out of there and let it all blow over. My father sent a helicopter for us and we left soon after I was cleared," he finished, nervously waiting for her response.

Alex had been longing to hear from him, for any kind of explanation. Months had passed and he had her number all this time.

"You could have called me, as a friend Xav. It would have been nice to know you were ok. I understand that what happened to us was so insane, and there was nothing really between us," she said firmly.

"No, that's not true Alex. There is something between us, you know there is. That's why I'm here."

Alex had been trying hard not to look into his blue eyes but now she did and was lost. At that moment the waitress arrived with the forgotten tapas and placed it carefully around the table.

"Let me know if you need anything else. I'm just over there," she smiled at Xavier, then pointed to the bar where a number of people were looking towards them.

"Are you more famous than before?" Alex asked.

"My television show has sold to the US and they are playing it now. I was away doing the voice-overs in English. It seems that my little brush with scandal did not hurt my career. Maybe it is you they are looking at, not me?" He made it clear he was paying her a compliment.

"I doubt that," laughed Alex. "Not when I'm sitting

next to you. That waitress is staring daggers at me, she would give anything to be in my place."

"I am not interested in any other woman," Xavier insisted, taking her hand.

"I've started filming my new series in the Caribbean," he went on. "The forecast was tropical storms for the next week so I decided to fly to London. I'm so glad you would see me."

"Xav, you can't have come all the way here just for me? You're mad!" Alex protested.

"I don't think so, you are all that I can think about," he said sincerely. "I had to see if what we felt for each other was real, but I know for certain. I am supposed to be exactly here, right now, with you."

She could do nothing but look at him. All her life she had dreamed of something elusive, mysterious, romantic. She figured it was impossible, but here it was in the flesh. She was totally overwhelmed.

"I am starving, Alex," he said, looking straight at her. "But not for this food."

He raised his hand to attract the attention of the waitress, who was still staring.

"I think we need the bill, thank you."

Outside the restaurant, the rain was relentless.

"Where to?" Xavier asked.

"Just round the corner, quickly run!"

They rushed through the rain to the front door, while Alex fumbled in her bag for the keys. They entered the cottage and stripped off their outer coats, shaking out the rain and laughing at their soaked appearances, breathless after the short sprint to the house.

In the tight proximity of the hallway, Xavier turned to look at Alex. He held her face in his hands and kissed her deeply. No words could have conveyed the message in that kiss, and he knew immediately that he had been right all along.

For Alex it was just the same as before, and in seconds she didn't know what way up she was. Her heart was thumping and she was weak at the knees, as he pressed up against her as they merged into each other. She reached for his hand and led him up the staircase to the bedroom. Regardless of her misgivings, there was no going back. She wanted this man, she could not deny it.

Xavier sat on the bed and gently pulled Alex towards him. He looked up at her while she carefully removed her dress, a goddess was revealed before him. He was desperate to show her how much he wanted her but he needed to be patient. He slowly removed her underwear, then drew her naked onto the bed, quickly stripping off his clothes to join her, his body on fire.

Alex now knew what it was like to ache for someone, but he wouldn't be drawn into her yet. He gently kissed her all over, caressing her breasts and down between her legs. She was grabbing at his hands, urgent for more, but he continued with his intimate touching until she was pulling him into her. Now it couldn't be stopped and when he finally entered her, she gasped at the feel of him and he lost himself completely inside her body.

The whole night they made love, this wasn't just sex and they both knew it. They joined themselves together in every way; at times finding their heads at the foot of the bed, as they twisted together through the night.

Hours later, Xavier was still gently running his finger along her arm as she finally slept. He wrapped her up closely to him and cradled her sleeping body. There was no way he could rest like her, he needed to think. She had been living in his thoughts for months and now she was real and right here. He didn't want it to ever change, he wanted her to be with him always. He felt amazingly complete.

His mother had pushed him together with Victoria while they all relaxed in her husband's Martinique villa after the trauma of Lassay. Victoria was a great girl; he liked her enormously but when he was with Alex it was pure magic.

There was nothing to compare to how he felt about her.

Around 5.00am, he got up and went in search of coffee. In the early morning light, he could see their scattered clothes on the bedroom floor. He didn't try to get dressed, just went naked to the kitchen and searched for the coffee machine.

Alex appeared at the kitchen door in a silky gown. She looked tired and a bit dishevelled, but he thought that nobody had ever been more beautiful.

"Sorry I can't work your machine. I was going to make us coffee in bed," he smiled at her.

Alex felt shy which was ridiculous, she was a grown woman not a girl. Xavier was completely naked and it was hard not to just stare at him. She went to the coffee machine and he stood right behind her as if he were interested in how it worked, but leaning into her back. Her hands were shaking as she tried to fit the coffee pod.

"Let me, I'm good at this bit," Xavier offered, reaching round to fit the pod.

She placed the cup and as they waited, he began nestling his face into her neck.

"I won't be able to make this coffee unless you move away from me!" she insisted. He laughed and moved back a fraction.

Alex managed to make the coffees, despite the level of interference. They took them into the sitting room and sat opposite each other. Xavier looked at her and steadily held her gaze.

"I can't leave you again, Alex," he told her straightaway. "I want us to be together, we can find a way if we both want to."

"Xavier, what are you saying? This is madness, we both have lives and they are not even in the same country, let alone the same town," she reasoned. She could hardly be expected to concentrate on important matters when he was sitting there completely naked in front of her.

"Leave this," he indicated the life she had created. "Come with me, why not? Let's try to live our dream."

"I can't just walk out on my life, Xav," Alex resisted. "I have a job, a home, a family. I can't get on a plane tomorrow and leave, just like that."

"You only have one life Alex, it's not a rehearsal."

"What time is your flight?"

"Midday tomorrow. I will need to be at Heathrow for 10.00am at the latest," he replied, then insistently. "Alex, please think about it. Think about the life we could have together, that's all I ask."

***

Xavier went to collect his things from the hotel, and Alex took the day off to plan a special meal for their last night together. The parting was with them all day, but she was determined not to be sad. She was flattered he had asked her to run away with him; perhaps she would see him again, after all they both had reason to be in Lassay.

A few weeks here and there seemed more likely to her, than some fantasy of falling in love with a famous television star. It was an impossible daydream. She had a life already, with responsibilities and plans of her own. Or did she? Was she so happy with her life? Too much introspection made her crazy, she must stop this!

The evening was perfect, they were happy and relaxed. Xavier did not ask her again to come with him, and they were content to spend one more wonderful night together before he had to go. The sex was incredible as she knew it would be. They clung together all night and made love with passion and fervour.

The taxi would take them both to Heathrow but Alex would stay in and return after dropping him off. She worked so hard to stop the tears that she could hardly speak, but Xavier seemed animated and was excited about getting back to work on the beautiful island of Martinique.

They kissed passionately on the pavement outside the terminal. He held her face close to his and looked into her soul. No words of love were spoken, it was not necessary. Alex turned back into the taxi so he would leave before she broke down completely.

"*Au revoir chérie*," he whispered after her, vowing he would try again after filming finished.

Alex looked back at Xavier as she drove away and waved goodbye. That was it then, over and done with, best not to think about it. Everyone knew long-distance relationships rarely worked out. The tears were rolling down her face as she looked aimlessly out of the window on the way back to her little cottage.

Her life felt empty suddenly. She had let the most wonderful opportunity that had ever come her way just pass, and now it was gone and she was alone. At that moment her phone rang and she rushed to answer it, thinking that it might be Xavier but it was John.

"Hi Alex, do you fancy going out tonight?"

"No. Not tonight, John. I'm not feeling great," she told him honestly.

"It's kind of important. Kevin and Melinda have invited us to the Ivy." He came straight to the point, clearly pleased with himself. "A couple dropped out, so they thought we might enjoy a last-minute invitation."

Kevin and Melinda owned the company John worked for. Alex knew how significant it was for him, even to be invited as an afterthought. This was an important mark of togetherness, to be acknowledged as a couple on the rise, and what she had wanted all those months ago. Alex had been seeing John now and again as a friend, so she wanted to be supportive of his big night.

"Ok, what time can you pick me up?" she decided. It would distract her from the endless tears and moping over Xavier.

"Is 7.30pm alright? Look if you're ill, maybe they can invite us another time," he said uncertainly.

"No, really, I'm sure I'll be fine by then." Alex felt ripped apart, everything was wrong.

She had a terrible hollow feeling from saying goodbye to Xavier at the airport. She could still breathe him in but he seemed somehow unreal and now he was gone. John was real, everything she understood, the life she envisaged. He was familiar and comfortable, just like her parents.

At 7.00pm there was a ring on her doorbell. Alex thought it was John early, as he often was, and she was almost ready accordingly. There was no John when she opened the door, instead she had to sign for a bunch of twelve perfect red roses and a letter.

She opened the envelope and read the message:

Here is an open ticket to Martinique. You are the woman of my dreams. Please make me the happiest man in the world. Come to me Alex, I'll be waiting for you.

Alex turned it over and the address was on the back of the card. She was reading the note again, when the doorbell rang and this time it was John. He seemed a bit hyped up instead of his usual stolid self, maybe nervous of the approaching dinner with Kevin and Melinda. Alex was glad to rush straight off, she didn't want John to see the flowers and definitely not the letter and ticket. You do this to yourself Alex, kept running through her head.

***

Kevin and Melinda Yeats had done well for themselves, dinners at the Ivy or Soho House were commonplace. Alex had heard about them but never met them. She was apprehensive, but for all the wrong reasons. She soon found this out to her cost, especially when Melinda turned out to be a small and overweight woman, with a sharp accountant's brain and little social grace. Kevin was a large, loud man who couldn't keep his eyes or his hands off Alex.

The foursome sat in the middle of the main dining room and ate wonderful food. Unfortunately, the atmosphere was less pleasing. Melinda complained, a lot. Kevin laughed too loudly and attracted tuts from other diners.

Just before the dessert, John tapped his glass with his knife and the tinkling noise gained all their attention. He walked round to Alex and knelt on one knee and in front of Kevin and Melinda, and everybody else dining, he asked her to marry him.

John produced an expensive-looking diamond ring in a red leather embossed box. No doubt to impress Kevin, she found herself thinking unkindly. Alex gazed around for a few seconds and took in the whole scene. No, this was not what she wanted. She was still young and she had only one life.

Alex picked up her bag, then without saying a word walked straight out of the dining room. John joined her at the cloakroom. She looked at the crestfallen expression on his face, but there was nothing left to say.

"No, John. No," was all she could manage, before walking out into the night.

***

It took only two days to hand in her notice and verify the ticket. Her mother took her to the airport, crying intermittently.

"Why? Why throw your future away for an adventure?"

Alex would never be able to make her understand, she finally knew exactly what she wanted and she was going for it. Her mother was kindly organising the flat and storage, so was in her own way, aiding and abetting her departure even though she disapproved. They said their goodbyes and Alex went through the airport procedure to the plane, ready to move towards her future.

***

Inspector Giles Bonet was on a tropical beach himself, on the other side of the world on the island of Réunion. He was sitting with his wife talking about his retirement. She had got her way in the end and dragged him off on holiday, but it had all been worth it.

This had been a fabulous break, just the two of them. Madame Bonet a changed woman with a healthy tan, brightly-coloured summer clothes and a few cocktails in her. They had re-kindled their own romance during the past week and for the first time in ages Giles felt young and alive.

Preview

Secret Identity

Deadly Romance on a Caribbean Island

By Lizzie Diamond

Alex Taylor is madly in love with Xavier de Verre and living her fantasy life on the island of Martinique. She is embracing the Caribbean beach paradise and writing her first novel, whilst Xavier films his television show.

Yvette de Verre-Müller generously offers the use of her yacht for the wrap party but she has her own agenda. Certain Alex is not the right woman for her son, she enlists the help of Lady Victoria de Savory, who is only too happy to play along with Yvette's Machiavellian schemes and secure Xavier for herself.

Assistant producer Maisie Levine heads to the island for a few days holiday before her colleague Sharlene Cooper, daughter of famous movie star Grant Cooper, arrives to disturb her peace. Finding a friend in Alex, she helps her prepare to face the formidable Yvette.

Local policeman Captain Eric du Pont is in charge of security and must keep track of the Hollywood crowd descending upon his tranquil island for the event of the season. When a guest disappears during the party, Yvette turns to Inspector Giles Bonet to find the truth and keep the secret.

Will Alex and Xavier overcome the plot to tear them apart or can love really conquer all?

Acknowledgement

I am grateful to my family and friends for their love and support but a special thank you:

To Taryn for saving my life without which this book would never have come to be.

To my dear friend Elizabeth for her support and encouragement.

To my daughter Amber who made it all possible.

To my mum who is my biggest fan.

About The Author

Lizzie Diamond

Lizzie Diamond creates mystery romance novels with a twist.

Lizzie lived in France for several years before returning to the UK.

She is married and has three grown-up children and a very large dog.

Printed in Great Britain
by Amazon

86797258R20161